THE MARTLET'S TALE

THе

NICHOLAS DELBANCO

marTLeT's TaLe

J. B. LIPPINCOTT COMPANY
PHILADELPHIA AND NEW YORK

To P. and to C.
together, apart

"A certain man had two sons. . . ."
—LUKE 15:11

"The martlet bird, footless, sleepeth in
wind, and dies when aye it land."

Contents

Part One   RHODES page 11

Part Two   ATHENS page 77

Part Three RHODES page 159

PART ONE

rHODes

_____

THE HOSPITAL OF RHODES squats on the hill that rises to be Monte Smith. Beneath the stunted pines they say that an Englishman walks. He looks for his home and for coal—mistaken, weightless, dead. Hung beads drive him blinded away; they call him Signor Smith.

Down past the white plaster walls and red roofs of the New Town, the streets of the Old Town of Rhodes curve and twist, and down past the wall lies the sea. Green sea circles land like a wreath; he will ever search lost and alone.

The Sun-God peopled Rhodes and guards his children still. Dawn winds from Turkey slip through the sharp leaves of tangerine trees and climb up the walls of the city, the grey standing fortress and streets. Dawn sends the dead Signor Smith up the mountain to sleep. He came first with invading Italians, was always named "Signor." Cocks crow, the muezzin calls, and his few faithful turn. The beaches are walled in with stone.

13

With winter come the never-ending rains. A strong sirocco blows clouds like whitecaps through the sky; the water on the rocks pours down to meet the water of the sea, and only a little, always-changing line of scum divides the sand that the sea has made wet from the sand that is soaked by the sky. The sky looks like dirty, wet wool, and the Sun-God floats drowned in his sea.

In every poor hillock, Smith saw a coal hill; he dug on the mountain and died. They buried him under a cross, but the townspeople hear him in wind. Feet dance on the hospital roof, where rain-water washes him clean.

When the never-ending rains end, it is early spring. Waves slap on the stones of the harbours and beaches, manacled to shore; the orange and lemon and Judas trees bloom, and the long yellow hospital squats beneath a sky of brass reflecting the glare of the sun. The heat tastes like brass in the mouths of the patients; the dead Englishman takes his tea.

He whispers, they say, wakening cocks, with grief that he cannot return. The mountain is his every night; the wind both his warden and host. Plaintive, he fills the night sky.

The hospital has two floors. On the second stretch the wards where the workers and poor peasants lie; on the first floor, where it is coolest, there are a few private suites shadowed by the great pines of the garden, and there is one waiting room.

Six or seven people stood in the waiting room: old

people, coal-eyed, dressed already in black. When Sotiris entered, they rushed at him, jabbering:

"Find out where the money is."

In the flock and hover, Sotiris knew an aunt, an uncle, and a doctor—the rest were friends, perhaps, or far-off relatives. The uncle, fat and embarrassed in a tight, black coat, drew Sotiris aside and told him, secretly:

"She can't live long, you know. Find out where the money is."

Then a nurse opened the door to the waiting room, noticed Sotiris, and smiled.

"She will see you now, Mr. Procopirios."

While the others drew back and grew silent, Sotiris followed her into the room where his grandmother lay.

She was old, Orsetta Procopirios. Her sons were raising the calf for her eightieth birthday. Her husband was twelve years dead. Four months before, in her great old age, she had collapsed with a stomach sickness, and, because she was very rich, and because her sons were important, all the doctors of Rhodes had watched over her, had cut into her swelling belly, and had kept her living.

Four months she had lain on her back, dribbling bile. As the liquid of her sickness stretched her belly, Orsetta Procopirios grew small; the skin that was tender on her great growing belly fell folded and creased to her back. The skin of her forehead fell in wrinkles to her eyes, and what she saw from her eyes was not the four white walls of the hospital room, but balconies and large, firelit halls;

she saw her husband in a wheel chair, bundled into coats even through the summer, wearing sheepskin, keeping the windows and doors closed and bolted, the fire burning so that death could not enter and surprise him. It came, and surprised only her.

Then the doctors said, with grave faces, that she no longer had acute peritonitis, that the operation had, therefore, been a success, but that she now had peritonitis that was chronic. At that, Orsetta Procopirios screamed at the doctors and the nurses and her family that they were trying, one and all, to murder her for money, and she would listen to no one but turned all day in her bed. The next day, through a visitor, because she felt the longing and the visitor was flattered, she smuggled a note that commanded a basket of pears to be brought from her arbours. Wide-eyed and frightened, Anna-Maria, the sister and servant of the wild old woman, smuggled pears in through the hospital, then, and Orsetta Procopirios ate of them greedily.

The doctors found her shivering on her side, lying on top of the bed because the bed sheets hurt so much. She was lying in her vomit and in great pain with the attack, but she would not call for help from any nurse or any doctor.

They operated on her again, and again they saved her life, but now they told the family that grandmother Procopirios could not possibly live long. And so the family tried very hard to please the angry old woman, and the family was very pleased when she asked to see Sotiris.

When he came in, she was lying on her back with her knees drawn up, and a bib tied to her neck to catch the bile.

"Yásou, yayá," Sotiris said, "I hope I find you well."

Grandmother Procopirios struggled upward to him on her pillow and said, in a hoarse voice:

"Have they fatted the calf for my eightieth birthday?"

"Yes, yayá," he answered.

"And how many days until then?"

"A few months, yayá. Time enough for you to get well in, and then there will be a big party."

Sotiris would have gone on speaking of his father's preparations, but the old woman waved her hand, suddenly angry at his not knowing how many days.

"Don't speak of it to me. Murderers, my sons. And two of them have married whores."

There were three sons: Manos, the youngest, the fat man standing outside; Triphon, the eldest, living in America now; and Apelis, the father of Sotiris. Apelis, too, had lived in America, and when he had lived there, before he came back and was married, grandmother Procopirios had gone off to visit him, promising to take much money along. It was far too much money to take out of the country, and the customs house had found her out, had forbidden her to take more than a little. The officer at the customs had taken time with her bags, not listening to her speeches but inspecting the bags very carefully. He had called another officer over, and, from the look in their eyes, from the way they had reached for the dress where the money was hidden, Orsetta Procopirios was sure they had been warned. And from that day the wives of Manos and Triphon were whores.

"What may I do for you, yayá?" asked Sotiris, hoping to please her and to make her stop.

"Do, little Sotis? I tell you. Do you think I cannot hear through these walls? Do you think I do not know what they are wishing? We must go, together, from here to Charaki, today."

He could not speak before she had started again.

"No. I know what you are thinking. You think, like the others, I cannot live long. But ninety-seven days—what are you, twenty years? I will have four times that! I tell you, little Sotis, little twenty years, I'll live to eat my calf when it is fatted. I have more money than they have ever thought."

With that, she lay back, tired, and Sotiris noticed that the sheets, when she breathed, moved only over her chest, that she was not breathing with her stomach, and that there the sheets lay still. He loved her, still, and thought of her once having given him the present of a donkey to ride within her vineyards and down the village roads. Then, ten years before, she had been seventy, and she had been kind to little Sotis, her newly dead husband's namesake.

Sometimes, at night, while the gulls cried and circled, she would tell Sotiris of the wars his father and grandfather fought, sing him a fighting song, and he would sit and listen, quiet, by her side, fingering gently an old bayonet that she had kept and let him touch. Sometimes, by day, she would ride with Sotiris through the vineyards, where the workers would bow and rush to bring choice grapes to the old woman and the little ten-year-old boy, and he would look at her and laugh.

But Orsetta Procopirios soon stopped going out into the vineyards, for she grew afraid, afraid of her workers and night, afraid of the rabbits and heat. Sotiris would go out alone after grapes, then, and come back hours later, leaving his donkey and shouting into the house: "Look, yayá, I am here, and nothing happened!" while the woman ran to him and held his brown head tightly to her breast, for still she was taller than he.

The walls were of white plaster, and the grey floor, cold. Sotiris heard a nurse.

"Yayá, it cannot be so bad in here," he said.

But Orsetta would not answer; merely she kept saying, "We must go," over and over again, in the rhythms of her pain.

"It loses in the telling," chortled Manos to his wife, "but figure this, my dear. A fisherman, out in his boat, collapses with a heart attack, alone. He wakes an hour later, one hand on a langouste pot, and aching in the side. He rows his boat back to the shore, beaches it, alone, walks the two-mile road to home, falls upon his bed, and dies. The son is baking bread."

When Sotiris walked out of the room, the waiting people circled him.

"How is she?" asked Eleni, his aunt, anxiously.

"Very well, thank you," said Sotiris. "How are you?"

But his aunt did not answer. She gave him an angry look, and then, when someone laughed, she gave the angry look to Manos her husband, who stood near, who repeated stories now, and spent most of his time with friends in the cafés.

"Out with it," his aunt said. "Did she tell you?"

"She told me she wanted to leave."

The doctor came forward to call it impossible; no patient suffering from peritonitis should ever be moved, and a journey, even by ambulance, would almost surely be fatal. As Sotiris restated the old woman's wish, however, Eleni, his aunt, said that it was clear they were going for the money, and the doctor swallowed and said that he had to confer.

A few minutes later, the three doctors who had operated on Orsetta Procopirios came in, together with the doctor who had gone off to fetch them, and they said, smiling, that, as it was the dying woman's wish, and as she could not survive much longer, yes, they would consent, upon consideration, to let the hospital ambulance take her wherever she wanted. Sotiris said, of course, she wanted to go back to Charaki. The doctors said, of course. And so it was arranged that he and his grandmother should go in the ambulance back to Charaki, the village where she lived, and the doctors wished them well.

"Find out where the money is, boy, we must know soon," his uncle repeated and left.

Alone, in the waiting room, Sotiris wondered if he would get to his grandmother's treasure, or if it existed at all. He knew that Triphon had come once from America in answer to Orsetta's call. She had told him, so they said, where the money was hidden, and had given him the right to what he might find—but when he dug where she had told him, there was nothing: none of the millions of drachmas and gold candlesticks that were hers from the sale of her houses and land. He had continued digging, underneath a lightning-crippled carob tree, until there were great piles of rubble on the ground; he had followed the roots of the carob tree all the way down until he had reached rock, and there was nothing but rock. Sotiris remembered still the way, at dinners, his uncle's handsome face would go ugly with the strain of having to hold back his anger, of having to seem a success. Triphon had returned to New York, laughed at and proud, unpursued; he had been silent four years and had written again only because of the news of Orsetta's urgent illness.

They said that the same thing had happened, later, to Manos, that he had also dug and dug, finding nothing, and kept silence.

Sotiris had never heard anyone say that Apelis, the favourite, was told where to look and had failed; his father did not fail.

Sotiris had stopped stuttering at the age of ten. He no longer pulled at his tongue; he no longer dreamed he was deaf. But still he could sing more than speak.

The grandmother, Orsetta, lay curled beneath the sheets, running her tongue around in her mouth and pushing at her cheeks. She thought of how much her grandson looked like her husband; she thought of how she had looked with her husband when they were married; she thought of all the rooms in the house, of what they were like, and then she remembered the firelit hall where her dying husband would sit; she thought of his sheepskin and keys.

When Sotiris came back to tell her she could leave, her voice, as she spoke, was a whine: "No, I will not go. You are making me go. You want only my money, and I will not go."

"Yayá," said Sotiris, "don't be angry with me. You are the one who wanted to go, and it will do you good to be back in your home again. Anna-Maria is there, and she will take good care of you."

"Anna-Maria is a fool, and would have killed me with those pears."

But she thought to herself that, with only Anna-Maria, she could do as she wished. Calmer, thinking of her house and of the festival there, in ninety-seven days, she called for the nurse to come and make her ready, to prepare. Still muttering beneath her breath, "I will not go, I won't tell," she shivered when the nurse pulled back her sheets.

"A man went into town to buy some cheese. He saw a bar of soap and asked: 'How much does that stuff cost?' 'Ten drachmas a kilo,' the shopman said. He thought that cheap enough for cheese and said: 'Give me a slice, then, two drachmas worth.' The shopman sliced; he paid. On the way home, he started eating it; the soap foamed in his mouth, but he was so stingy he kept on eating and said: 'Don't even bother to foam. I paid for you, and I shall eat you now.' "

Stavros threw back his head and laughed; he'd told the story before, but laughed again, laughed at it every time. He plucked at his short beard; he had been making cheese. His hand was sticky with the liquid cheese and spread it on his beard; pointing, he laughed again. He held his arms up high and shook; the other shepherds laughed. The thickened milk dropped from the wooden ladle in his hand and dribbled down his open shirt; the vat of cheese in front of him shook, liquid lapping at the sides; the balls of drying cheese stirred in their plaited baskets as he laughed.

"I paid for you, and I shall eat you now," he roared, plunging his hands down in the vat again and thickening the milk. The lambs and kids stood at a distance, bleating, sounding bells; just outside the fold, Valeria looked on. Valeria was Stavros' single calf, the calf Apelis had selected for his mother's birthday; Stavros, Apelis' shepherd, had been rearing her.

He had reared her from birth, had cared for her three months. Four months before, four weeks before she had been born, Apelis had bought the next calf, upon approval, from a neighbour who kept cattle; Apelis pastured only sheep and goats. When, therefore, the neighbour's first cow calved, Stavros went to look at it and take it back with him. Valeria (he called the calf Valeria, thought it a noble name) had already been licked, cleaned and warmed by her mother; Stavros arrived too late. He would have much

preferred to rub the calf himself with dried grass and
with straw. He hunched his shoulders, spat. "Cow!" he
announced to the neighbour's watching shepherd, "you are
far more a cow than those you tend; you wear a buck-goat's
beard. She is not to know her mother; she has to stay with
sheep, my sheep and goats; we do not want her lonely, left
alone. Better she should never know, and think herself a
sheep." And with that, careful, proud, he took Valeria
(just whispering, not saying the name aloud) and re-
rubbed her himself.

When the mother cow gave yellow, near-pink milk, the
rich milk needed by her baby, Stavros took it into a pail
and fed the calf himself, making his fingers teats. Valeria
sucked upward, turning for a teat, and had to be coaxed to
drink down from the pail, had to be convinced. Stavros
spent long hours with her, dipping his fingers in milk and
bringing her mouth to his fingers, wiggling, and then to
the pail, weaning her from birth.

He carried her to his own sheepfold and fed her pru-
dently and well, strengthening her quickly, providing
stolen milk.

The drive to Charaki lasted an hour, the siren inter-
mittent, their procession, slow. Great white acacia trees
scudded past the ambulance window like clouds, and
Orsetta Procopirios, closing her eyes, breathing only in the
chest, rattled in her throat as if dying. The black hairs of
her moustache were like ink lines on the paper of her face.
Her chin was black with hair. The ambulance bounced on
its bad springs through the New Town and out into the

open, badly paved road, and, with each shock, a little spot of black rolled down around her eyes. Orsetta Procopirios had not liked to admit that her hair had turned white; she had painted it, since her husband's death, with a black paste that the peasants said was good for giving colour and for curing baldness. The paste was a mixture of black boot polish, powdered dry fig leaves, and two yolks of egg, and ever since she had started to think of herself as a peasant again, Orsetta Procopirios had painted herself with the paste. Now she was sweating with the strain of the trip and the heat, and it ran in great black drops down her face, leaving little lines of paint and meeting with the bile in the corners of her mouth.

"My trees will be dead," said the old woman suddenly.

"What's that, yayá?"

"My trees will be dead," she repeated, looking at the green and white and purple treetops in the window. "St. Constantine's day will go this year."

The owners of fig and pomegranate trees get engaged to their trees on St. Constantine's day. They hang wreaths of oleander and wild marjoram across the branches: the trees therefore know that their owners still live, and, joyful, they bear fruit.

"St. Constantine's day will go, has gone," she said, "and I am not engaged to them. They will think I am dead."

Orsetta shivered, thinking of the death of her orchards, and she said, without looking at Sotiris: "Boy, rub my feet for me, would you? They are cold."

Sotiris bent toward her and took her feet in his hands. They were old and deeply wrinkled, dirty, with sweat in the wrinkles; she had not let herself be washed by any nurse. Sotiris told himself that this was his grandmother, and was not disgusted. But, feeling that the smell might make him sick, he tried not to think about what he was doing, and looked away from her out of the window.

"My trees will have died out of sorrow," she said, still trying to punish Sotiris for coming with her on her journey. "But everyone else will be glad."

Through the window, Sotiris could sometimes see the far-off, deep-green sea, but more often he watched the long road to Malona wind through the valleys of grass and grape vineyards where stone and metal windmills stood instead of trees. A few farmers had readied sails, so that their rows of windmills slapped loud circles in the wind, but most of the grey-brown windmills were useless and abandoned now—windmills that the Italians had once imported by the hundreds to raise water from the wells, windmills with the sign "Made in Chicago" slowly rusting, their gun-metal spokes turning slowly, with muddled nests of storks upon their stone.

Up clinging in a tree, in the small shaken crook of a branch, Sotiris sat and waited for his food. It was a picnic; down below, too far to reach, too far to climb (how had he gotten there, the others called and called to him he had to hurry down, but how, he cried, how make the slightest move?) and all the food was gone. He was just six years old. He stuttered and they thought it fear; he called out for his food. They would not pass it up to him; he could not clamber down, nor jump. And then his father walked away, his brother next to him, the others too, and he was left to slip and tumble down alone.

The ambulance bounced through Archangelos, with its houses stretching back into the fields, but near Malona they had to stop. There had been an accident. Two farmers, one holding a frightened ass hard by the bridle and the other standing in front of his truck, stood in the middle of the road, screaming so loudly that Orsetta struggled upward to see. She saw, near the two men, on the side of the road, a pregnant ass lying with its stomach hanging out, in a large lake of blood that covered the grass that the hurt ass was trying to eat. Orsetta felt her stomach turning at the sight, and she called out to Sotiris:

"We must go. I do not want to see this."

But the ambulance had stopped. The doctor explained that he was sorry for the delay, but a wounded ass, and especially a pregnant one, might make all the difference to a poor farmer, and he, the doctor, must see if he could help. Again, he was sorry for the delay, but it should not take long, and the chance to rest, he hoped, would help. When the doctor hurried off, Sotiris could hear what had happened.

Coming home from the market, the one man had driven his truck into the side of the pregnant ass, who had been too slow to get out of the way and too stupid to be scared by the horn. Now she lay on her side, aborting, blood-bathed, with great liquid shudders of breath, with the flies already black upon her entrails. The other ass had almost gone frantic trying to reach her, but the farmer held the frightened ass firmly, and the two men argued on until the doctor, who had gone to look at the wounded animal, came back and told them that nothing could be done, that, to settle it, they would have to see a judge. The ambulance started again.

They reached Malona quickly and turned for the road to Charaki. Orsetta Procopirios owned much of the land on either side of this road, and she raised herself to see her silver-grey olive groves, her twisted fig and lemon trees black against the sky. The trees took her mind from the destroyed she-ass, and she said: "Sotiris," no longer using the pet name, Sotis, "I wish to talk with you. Come closer, I cannot shout."

Sotiris leaned forward until he smelled the face of his grandmother and saw the paste in her hair.

"You think, because I have asked you to get me away, that I'll tell you where the money is hidden. But now I can do as I wish, I will not go back, and you have helped me without knowing. You should have asked before."

She laughed and said: "I have told Manos and Triphon once, too. And my money still is mine, little Sotis."

Orsetta Procopirios stopped talking then, because the road through her vineyards became only dirt, and the ambulance, pitching and bumping downhill toward the sea, took everything out of her face but the black lines of paint.

Apelis Procopirios, fifty-six years old, could still stand like the amateur boxer he was once, sucking in his stomach, and he still could lift crates full of cloth in his clothing stores. He was five feet, seven inches tall. He brushed a mane of machine-grey hair back from his temples: his wife, Nicoletta, was dead.

"You there, Andreas," he called to his son.

Andreas, the first-born, looked up. Apelis was trying to fit a carrier of cloth into place on the wall, and he could not both lift and guide it.

"I want you here, quickly," he said.

Yards of deep brown cloth were wound onto a metal spool, so that the cloth could be spiralled and shown: the ends of the spool fitted into the wall. Carefully, they steadied and fixed it; one side, then the other.

"Good," said Apelis, and stepped back, making sure. He was wealthy enough to stop work, but he came every day to the stores, spending the day in checking accounts, selling

and buying, redoing. Andreas, twenty-four, managed one
of the stores.

"What is the time?" asked Apelis. "Is it three-thirty
yet?"

"Past that, near four o'clock."

"Good," said Apelis. "By now Sotiris must know what
she wants."

He had named his first-born in honour of Orsetta's
father; he had named his second son Sotiris, in honour of
her husband. Because of this, because Manos and Triphon
had no children, and because of the way that he was,
Apelis and his family had always been favourites, and now
Orsetta, so they said, would offer them her treasure. Signor
Smith had whispered from the hospital's high roof: no
doubt at all.

And he thought to himself: "It is mine."

Charaki is at the end of the road that leads from Malona
to the sea. At the end of the road stands a grocery store,
which is also a café and the place of the village council;
fifteen houses fan out on either side of the store and arch
along a horseshoe bay. There is no church or telephone;
Malona is near enough for both. The stone and mud
houses are all fifty feet from the water; a white pebbled
beach lies between.

There are sunsets on the water where the sea swallows
up the sky and gives it back again, washing it red and
purple and yellow. Then the white stones of the beach
catch fire, burning red and purple and yellow until the
sun falls lower, the stone turns to ash, and the fire creeps

into the sea. Men sit with no light on their faces and listen
to terns cry and circle, slicing the sky as they hover, swoop,
and dive with a low moan for fish that the men cannot
see. Sometimes a man will break silence to beat his arms
and curse at the terns for catching fish, and sometimes the
men sit close together, huddled, to talk of their past and
their future now that the big boats can stay out on water
for weeks and have taken away all their trade.

Past the last houses on either side of Charaki, the beach
runs on and up into hills that are blue in the daytime with
violets, yellow with thistle and weeds and aloe. Purple grey
rocks like rain clouds hold up the hills, and only a few
scraggling trees grow. But there are many scallops in the
shallows of the water, and here the gulls catch scallops and
break them open on the rocks. The sound of the birds
killing food will carry in wind to the men on the walk: at
night there is always a wind.

At night, the last man will come in from the bay, where
he has grown cold and tired setting out and hauling
langouste pots, for there are hardly any langouste any
more, and the men will say "yásou" and "good night,"
going inside to sleep. Those who are too old to sleep, the
old men, sit beneath a sky that grows heavy with wind,
waiting until they too are tired and ready to go into houses.
They have no need to get up early or to go to wives: for
them, the night ends twice.

Sotiris' mother died when he was born; she had been very
weak. He had few ways of recognizing her: one picture
near the table of the dining room, her profile and a peas-

ant dress; a closet full of clothes, where he would hide sometimes and burrow in the smell of tangerine wood and thyme; a piece of golden jewelry, and many necklaces; the stories that Yannis, her one cousin, told, expansively, of how she led the village dance and how they courted her; Andreas' vague rememberings, for at her death he had been four, and always spoke about the smell of cooking and a song. Yannis tried to sing it once when he was very drunk, but could remember only the beginning of a verse; it was a lullaby, he said. My baby sleeps to get his fill of sleep, he sang, and, helpless, had to stop.

Apelis neither remarried nor took another woman—but with Nicoletta dead, he bought another, larger house. Sotiris thought this must explain her absence from the rooms. He looked like her, some people said, he had her nose and mouth. But, with Yannis once, he walked back to his mother's house, the house where he was born, and walked around the walls, not recognizing them.

Because of stuttering he sang, and all the instruments were his, bouzoúki and guitar, santoúri and reed flute, each of the island songs. He sang them at his ease, and, at his ease, could speak.

The people of Charaki stood in front of the grocery store and circled the stopped ambulance. The men without work pressed close, like gulls that come to mate or to punish an offending gull, filling the air with their cries, their wings beating all the same circle. As Sotiris stepped out, fifteen or twenty men tried to claim kinship:

"Cousin, how are you?"

"You remember me, Sotiris, how was school?"

"And the family, your father, how is he?"

Sotiris had come to the village less and less often. Years before, he had loved to ride on his grandmother's land, and to swim in the soft, warm water, and to lie with his friends on the rocks; but lately, as the village grew poor and his grandmother more and more distant, not wanting family near, he had avoided Charaki.

It was too hot to stand in the afternoon sun, and he wanted to get to his grandmother's house. They lifted her, groaning, out of the car; the circle of women and children and old ones fell back.

"Here, let me help you," said a man with a fingerless hand, one of the men without work, turning to the stretcher.

"No, thank you," said Sotiris. "We are fine."

"But cousin, don't you know me?" asked the other, hurt. "I am Alexis Panayotis. You remember."

Nobody dared to speak with Orsetta; she lay on the stretcher and smiled.

Her house stood next to last in the row of houses to the left of the grocery store. It was a little, rectangular house, built, like all the others, with walls of dark grey stone, with a dark, triangular, slate roof. A black chimney pipe opened out of the roof. A fence, the only one in the village, built of four-foot-high rock from the hills, covered with barbed wire and bits of broken glass, protected the house from the walk. Coils of barbed wire stretched, clinging, from the chimney to the doorstep and wound like a black poisoned ivy up the walls. The house was set back from the beach, and, across the twenty feet before the fence, there was nothing but sand, stone, and rubble. Every two weeks, Orsetta ordered bottles broken, slivered tin, and threw it on the ground.

Orsetta Procopirios looked at the house and the protection of the wire, and she thought of how they had told her, at the hospital, not to expect to return to Charaki. Ninety-seven days; she smiled. The nurse was drowned in sheets. Orsetta thought about being again in her familiar home, not living with her children as they had asked and not in the strange, white-walled hospital room. She said, propping herself on her elbows:

"It has not been destroyed, at least."

Inside the house, waiting, nervously, Anna-Maria Charaiambos, servant and sister, watched Orsetta being carried up the path. Anna-Maria, too, was small, with the same bird eyes and face of weathered wood, but even in her health she did not possess the same strength. Younger by six years, the last of the six children of whom Orsetta was third, and all of whom were dead, except for these two and a brother, mad Kyrillos, dying somewhere near Athens, Anna-Maria, the baby of the family, had been Orsetta's care when their mother was busy. Since the family was poor, and the mother nearly always busy working in the kitchen or the vegetable gardens or fields, the two sisters had to spend much time together, the other four children being boys and allowed to run free from the house.

Anna-Maria loved her elder sister very much. When Orsetta escaped to walk with her friends, little Anna-Maria would run after them, short-legged and stumbling, asking to share in the game. And when, a little later, Orsetta grew powerful and round-hipped, with hard breasts and long, black hair that made the boys look and call to take her walking, chaperoned, by the beach, Anna-Maria would stand and push at her chest and her stomach, push them into shape when the light struck her window so that it was a mirror, and she would try to think of the things that Orsetta said to the boys, and of what they would do together.

Once, walking alone in the woods, along a secret path and up to a rock where she and her sister had often gone together to lie in the sun and dream about being princesses, Anna-Maria, with no reason to be careful, stumbled on a root in the sudden sun of the clearing and heard a male voice asking: "Who's there?" When she called out her name in a reflex of fear, she heard the man curse and then heard the loved voice of her sister telling her to go quickly. Anna-Maria turned and ran crashing back through the bushes, but she had seen and could not forget the naked back of the man, and she had heard and could not forgive the sharp, surprised voice of her sister.

She never dared talk to Orsetta about it, for even then her sister was closed into herself and easily angered, but when, a year later, the beautiful Sotiris Procopirios from the large, land-owning family of Malona came more and more often to call for Orsetta, and when, finally, the rich parents of Sotiris swept into the house to talk of a wedding, Anna-Maria could not contain herself, and she would make up wild, proud stories to tell to her friends; she would tell about Sotiris and Orsetta with always a little shiver of love and guilt while she talked.

Orsetta was married and went to live in Malona. Anna-Maria would sometimes visit her shyly, wondering at the hugeness of her house, and there, in Malona, one night at dinner, as the servants offered food, she noticed that the eyes of an army friend of Sotiris' were on her as the eyes of other men had been on Orsetta. She dropped her water glass; it broke. When she asked her sister, blushing, for his name, Orsetta smiled and said that it was Panos Charaiambos, and that he was neither stupid nor poor.

Almost three years later, when she was nineteen, Anna-Maria was married to Panos Charaiambos, and together they moved to the capital city of Rhodes, where Panos became a master tailor and opened a shop and fared well. In the nights, in the little room over the shop, Anna-Maria would always remember to thank her sister, in her prayers, for having introduced her to her husband, and then she would get into bed and kiss him, with always a little shiver of shyness and of gratitude.

After forty years of marriage, Panos Charaiambos died, leaving her with no children. Anna-Maria Charaiambos put on black clothes and closed up the tailor's shop and went to live with her sister in the big, spreading house overlooking Malona. She acted as a nurse to Sotiris Procopirios, who was dying of cancer. Beautiful and diseased, he died soon, and his widow, too, put on black and went into mourning. She sold all of her houses and the land; she blackened her white hair with paste; visited by friends no more, she no longer drank wine. The two sisters lived together in the little house in Charaki that had belonged to the Procopirios family as a beach house, and there the one sister watched over the other; there, they spent twelve years.

The gentle Anna-Maria Charaiambos had dragged herself through the days when Orsetta was in the hospital, but she had been too timid to visit her often. Her face had crumbled away under small, brimming bird eyes, encrusted eyes that scarcely saw, until it had come to look, through her worry, once more like her sister's sick face. When finally the note came that said how much better Orsetta was, and that she wanted pears, Anna-Maria had gathered them herself, fumbling and joyous, smuggled them inside. When she found out what it was she had done, she did wakeful penance for nights. So now she stood anxiously in the house and awaited her sister's greeting.

"Hello, Anna-Maria."

"Orsetta, how are you?"

Sotiris noticed in the silence that the hills of Charaki were full of cicadas, and that their humming was loud in his ears.

"Well, well, I am well. And you?" asked Orsetta, looking round at her house.

"Oh, I am well. I am glad to see you. It's good that you are here."

"Yes, yes," said the old woman curtly. "It is good to be home."

And she thought: "I've come home. They thought me dead, and I'm alive again."

Home was two rooms. A big front room faced out to the water, and was also the bedroom, living room and dining room; behind, there was a room for the kitchen and toilet, newly installed, at Manos' expense, and never used. In the big front room, two beds stood at right angles to each other: one a half-cot with metal legs and no frame, belonging to Anna-Maria, lying along the wall of the door, and the other, larger, lying in the cool corner along the wall. The corrugated iron bedposts at the foot of Orsetta's bed cast shadow bars, at night, onto the head of the other bed, lining Anna-Maria's sleep-smoothed face. By night, the two women would lie in their beds, not talking, both looking out of the window and waiting for the small, rare clouds to drift across the window and the moon.

In a wooden closet by the wall, black clothes fell from wire hangers in a row. The clothes were so much alike that only the women themselves could tell the difference, and even then, sometimes, when one of them was tired and hung her dress in the wrong place, the other one would pick it next day off the hanger and put it on, only noticing the mistake by something slightly out of place, a button or a pocket or a bow.

Across the door, on the other side of the room, where the first Sotiris Procopirios had kissed his eager bride, then taken her torch-fishing for fun, stood a table carved of crooked olivewood, with straw-bottomed, olivewood chairs. On top of the table, out of place and dimmed by dust, but

holding all the light of the room, stood a pure white
marble figure of Pan playing upon his pipes. The statue,
rising two feet like a white ghost from the table's cheese-
cloth cover, reminded Orsetta of the time, long ago, when
food became so scarce and money so uncertain that the
peasants had more power than the rich. They would not
accept money for food, but traded instead for clothes and
for fine things. Orsetta, a landowner then, had been forced
to give away pictures and rugs and even a piano; her husband had been furious, had ordered fire set to farms; and
now, keeping the statue in her small, poor house, she felt
herself a peasant and clever at bargains.

A black shell phonograph lay in the shadow of the table.

"A man of Charaki was fishing with his friend. He saw
his own foot in the sea, and thinking it a fish, speared
it. It hurt him, and he said: 'To catch a fish is evil, for it
hurts.' "

"I would like to rest," said Orsetta Procopirios. "Sotiris,
put me on my bed."

Anna-Maria, the doctor, and the ambulance driver left
slowly when she asked them; the crowd shouted questions
outside. Sotiris, lifting his grandmother, took her to the
bed. The stretcher itself had been heavy, so that he had
not noticed how light she was, and his body jerked up with
a shock when he found her suddenly so easy to lift.

"Put me down easily, boy."

Straightening from the bed, he saw the ikons over her
head, and, next to them, he saw the yellowing, tin-framed

photograph of his father as a boxer, looking very fierce
and a little bit fat—with the writing, "Love, from Apelis,"
blurred across his chest.

She saw his look and laughed. "I will not give my money
to Apelis. Nor to Andreas, Triphon, Manos, none of them.
No, no, little Sotis—what would you think if I gave it to
you? And the money I kept for your father, well, it is
mine, also. He would have spent it; I give it to you. And
when I die," she said with self-pity, "I want you to come
here, and to take it all. Leave Anna-Maria food."

"I hope you will live very long, yayá."

"Yes, yes," said Orsetta. "I am sure that you do. Like
the others, you wish me to live. For ninety-seven days."

"I am very grateful," said Sotiris.

"Certainly."

As a token of truth, then, and faith, she told him to pull
away his father's photograph. Dead ants cascaded down.
Wedged into the frame, he found six five-hundred-drachma
notes. She gave them to him and announced:

"These are yours. Yes, yes, at the least, I would wish
you to stay. Live with them carefully and keep the treasure
safe as I have done. And you cannot look for it or have
it till I die."

Then Orsetta Procopirios made him go to the door, to
see if it was truly closed, and, lowering her voice, because
she did not wish the villagers to hear, she made him promise again not to look for the treasure or to touch it till she
died. When he had promised, she made him promise not
to tell anyone else, not to tell his father, even, and she
told him, quickly, that the money was buried three feet

underneath the phonograph, in the baked mud floor under the table, with the phonograph as marker and on
guard. Again, insistently, she made him promise not to dig
until she died, and not to tell anyone else, then ordered
him to leave, for she felt very weak. And she said to
herself:

"Does he believe me? He does not act like Manos or
Triphon. But I will not have him digging in my house."

As Sotiris stepped out of the gate, the crowd clustered
to him like flies. Behind him glittered glass. He heard
them ask if he had found out where the money was, if he
needed help, if everything was well, if his grandmother
was well, and then he heard Panayotis asking if he thought
he could now buy Chrysanthi. Chrysanthi was the first
girl Sotiris had known, when they were both sixteen, and
even though he had been nothing to her, and she had already been with many older village boys, with Panayotis
at least, the insult and the memory angered him, and he
felt himself growing red. He wondered, would he be able
to speak? So he told them, swallowing, to leave, because
his grandmother wished to sleep, and, waiting in the sun,
he watched them walk away. When they were gone, he
turned and walked back to the house.

Inside, he moved very quietly, so as not to wake his
grandmother, but she lay unmoving. He watched her and
wondered, for, since her illness, they said, she had not been
easily able to sleep. She and Signor Smith had talked the
long nights through, had wandered the slopes to the east.
Then Sotiris looked at the phonograph and stood for a

long time unmoving, thinking of the treasure. He tiptoed to the far wall where the old Italian bayonet hung. It was the bayonet that he had played with as a child, a souvenir of the war of liberation that Apelis, the hero, had given his mother, saying, as a joke, that now she would have something to protect herself with. Orsetta had not smiled but had taken the gift and placed it along a row of nails on the wall.

"Is he going to kill me?" she thought, lying still with her skin tingling, trying to pretend she was asleep.

Sotiris took the long, rusting metal knife from its rows of nails, and thought that he might easily kill his sleeping grandmother. Then he thought that perhaps she was not sleeping but dead, and then he walked quietly, holding the knife, from the room.

It was very hot outside, and he decided to go swimming. He walked to the left of the house, away from the village, down along the stones of the beach to the point where the bay of Charaki begins. Dead fish littered the stones, some newly washed up and still smelling, others that were brittle lines of bone.

Passing the skeletons of fish and the upturned striations of starfish feet, Sotiris rounded the tip of the point. He took off his shoes, and using the bayonet as support, climbed along the pitted volcanic rocks until he could no longer see Charaki. Then he took off his clothes and lay naked, feeling the hard, dry rocks beneath his back, and feeling, under his feet, where the water rose at high tide, the colder slime of algae.

He lay for a long time with hands thrown back above his head, feeling the sun fall full upon him and the heat rise from rocks to the small of his back. When the sun had brought sweat to his eyes, he slid down the rocks and eased into the water. He swam steadily and stopped, turning around with his face now focussed on the water, swimming slower so as not to distract himself with bubbles, seeing schools of angelfish. He thought that he saw an octopus and dove down to search, but the bottom was a tangle of coral and weed, so he surfaced again to swim back to the shore.

Lying in the sun, hands above his head, Sotiris wondered whether his grandmother lived, had lied, and why she wanted him to stay.

Rested, he took the bayonet in his hand, entered the water, and searched for sea urchins in the sand and low shelfing of the shore rocks. He found them clinging to rocks and speared through their intricate network of bone until he had four or five sea urchins skewered on his bayonet blade. Then he surfaced, leaving his deep-colored catch on the rocks, and dove again to search. When he had killed and carried up twenty or thirty, Sotiris came up out of the water, and, taking care to throw back the black, poisonous ones, and working carefully so as not to get the porcupinelike quills in his hand, he sliced open the sea urchins with his bayonet blade and sucked out their insides of bright orange caviar.

Soon he had littered the rocks with a garden of bright blue, green, and red bodies like cactus plants. When he had finished, he piled them together, dressed again, and wishing that he had brought lemon to make the caviar taste better, checking that the money still was there, circled out along the point and down to Charaki.

It was six o'clock when he came back, and the ambulance had to return. Sotiris told the doctor, who expected him to stay, that he, too, wished to leave, and left the bayonet inside Orsetta's gate. Watched by the crowd, pursued, they found the ambulance driver and started the trip to Malona. As they left, Sotiris thought he saw Chrysanthi standing in the crowd, but knew that he was wrong.

Orsetta Procopirios lay in her bed, thinking: "He would spend it all. He would eat up my money with whores."

Without grandmother Pro-
copirios, the ride back to Rhodes was a fast one. Sotiris
sat on the metal bed again; the doctor sat in front. Near
Archangelos, Sotiris saw the she-ass lying under flies, but
they did not stop. The doctor shook his head.

Sotiris thought of what the loss of the she-ass would
mean to the farmer. He thought of the law courts and of
who would, in the end, profit by the death of the animal,
if profit there could be. He remembered the way his
grandmother had been sick at the sight; he remembered
her old gift to him of his own donkey and wondered
whether it, too, was dead.

Near Archangelos, Sotiris saw the men and women
walking from an afternoon market, the men carrying slung
lambs and holding squawking chickens by the legs, one
man carrying a basket of turtledoves. He saw the bandan-
naed village girls with glistening skin, balancing sweetmeats or baskets of fruit on their heads, taking water and

wine to their men in the fields, carrying themselves well, so that the men might touch them with their hard, work-wet hands and say "Thank you"; girls going back to little white houses with pet sheep tethered outside, with green sprigs of sage and sweet-smelling thyme and mint hung from the walls, with hard little beds in the cool corner farthest from the door, waiting there until the sun would fall and heat would fall away, until the men would come home to eat and drink mastika, until perhaps a man would start a sad klepht song rising and falling in the evening wind, and the girls would bring their men to bed until morning.

Before seven, they had reached Rhodes. The ambulance slowed to a stop. Sotiris got out at the harbour of Mandraki, and having said his "Good night and thank you," standing in a tower's shade, he wondered whether Orsetta had lied and tricked him. He wondered how long he would have to wait before he could know; he thought of going back to Charaki to search and make sure. He decided for Dania again.

The walled Old Town of the crusaders is built out of stone. Sotiris walked away from the harbour, up the stone Street of the Knights, toward the Square of the Turkish Baths. He wondered whether his father would be proud or be angry and argue. Then he thought that he did not want to go home and tell everything to everyone; he remembered Dania; he thought of the treasure again, of his six crumpled notes, and of what he should say.

Shadowed by a mosque, Dania's house stood in darkness,

and the lights were on. He looked through the window, into the room where Mehmet Effendi sat sleeping.

Sleeping with his enormous head slumped back on his chair, Mehmet Effendi seemed small. His body was small, pear-shaped and old, but the skin of his face still was smooth, brown and soft, like the colour of his eyes and the colour of his hands. A thick white moustache grew from under his nose; a thick fringe of white hair still circled his head.

Mehmet Effendi slept much and drank in the cafés, and told fortunes when he needed money, but he no longer played the santoúri. Once he had been a very good santoúri player, and it was because of his gift that he had met Alexis Saranditis, the cellist, Dania's father. Alexis Saranditis, who was a lonely man with a buried wife and with only one child, had listened to Mehmet Effendi play his santoúri one night in a restaurant in Athens. He called the beggar Turk over to his table and spoke to him, haltingly, in Turkish. They drank together, and when Alexis Saranditis had finished his dinner, he suggested that they go out into the town together. They went, and the headwaiter in the restaurant smiled at them broadly.

They went first to a tavérna and heard bouzoúki singers and drank many bottles of retsina wine, talking of music. Alexis Saranditis said, sadly, that it was no good making music when there was no one now, no woman to hear you any more, and Mehmet Effendi laughed and said, laughing, that he knew of a woman who loved to make music. Alexis Saranditis looked up, laughed with him, and paid for the bottles of retsina wine.

In the rooms of the whore, Mehmet Effendi was very polite, and he insisted, playing host, that Alexis Saranditis should go first, and he assured Alexis Saranditis that it was perfectly safe, that the police made a weekly inspection. When Alexis Saranditis had finished and came again into the waiting room, Mehmet Effendi hurried in for his turn to the whore, smiling, bowing, unbuttoning his shirt, assuring his patron that it would not take a minute. The whore was half-Turkish, big-breasted, and Alexis Saranditis could hear her laughing loudly with her friend, Mehmet Effendi, in the other room, and then, after her laughing, he could hear only the loud sound of bedsprings.

The next morning, Alexis Saranditis brought the Turk to his daughter's hotel room, and he told her that Mehmet Effendi would live with them in Rhodes. Dania was eight years old then, and, even with her nurse, she had been frightened the night before because her father had not come to wish her goodnight and sweet dreams—and she was frightened, now, to see the great hook nose and dirty turban of her father's friend. But Mehmet Effendi was gentle with the girl, as Alexis had known he would be. Since he could not speak her language well, Mehmet Effendi played his santoúri to her instead, letting her feel the red velvet cover, letting her pluck at a string, smiling until they were friends.

Alexis Saranditis was often away on tour. As he was a lonely man, often, on his trips, he would call santoúri players to his table, would sometimes buy them a drink. There had, however, been something special in Mehmet Effendi, special enough to make Alexis feel good, just, and clever in bringing the Turk back to Rhodes and making him live in his house—and it was this thing in Mehmet Effendi that the little Dania learned to love. For Mehmet Effendi was mad.

His was not an angry, dangerous madness, but a gentle, smiling one: perhaps the hot Turkish sun had burned anger from his brain, or perhaps he had always been mad, a timid, soft, big-headed boy, staring wide-eyed at the insects in the dust and at the flies that flew across his face. Perhaps he had always lived smiling, in restaurants, with prostitutes, and at the kindness of others. Even the name, Effendi, was a name of mock respect; even his red fez faced high. For now, in his old age, he was gentle and mad, and he had put away his santoúri, which reminded him of begging, and he had put away his other bad memories.

Now, with food and a house to live in, he was happy all the time, and he would speak to Dania of having been a sailor or a singer or a priest, of having had a harem and having been a king. He would tell Dania endless and wonderful stories, smiling, as she took his arm and walked with him through the warrens and the markets of the Old Town. They comforted each other, and he taught her Turkish in their ten years together. Alexis Saranditis had been a long time dead, and had left them the house.

Café owners kept the old man near as a token of luck, and one day, sitting in a café, he had noticed Sotiris. Smiling, speaking tutored Greek, he came to Sotiris' table and made Sotiris buy him a drink. Mehmet Effendi sat, nodding his great slow head, smiling, touching Sotiris' hands.

Finally, he turned over Sotiris' cup to let the grounds run out into the saucer; he pursed his lips and looked into the coffee cup to read the writing there. Having studied the pattern of grounds, he looked at Sotiris, quickly serious:

"You will be very lucky. Follow me. Very lucky. A child of luck it is."

Sotiris had followed him slowly, not sure what to expect, wondering whether he had understood. After a long, twisted walk, the old Turk brought him to a house, and, smiling and bowing, left him alone with a girl in the dark living room. Then Sotiris had been sure, and he walked over to touch her, sure it was arranged. He had seen Dania before, walking, alone, in the Old Town, and had thought her very beautiful; excited, he had gone quickly to her.

She slapped him. Ordered out of the house, he went, ashamed and angry, stung, walking the alleys and streets, long into the night, returning again, late at night, slowly, losing his way, asking to speak with her. She came, and he told her how sorry he was, and, for Mehmet's sake, she forgave. That had been a year ago, and they promised to meet again soon. He came back the next day, as he was to come back all of the next days, and Mehmet Effendi met him, smiling, at the door, ushering him in.

Sotiris looked at the Turk sleeping now in the dark living room of the Saranditis house, and he wondered how old he was, if he were eighty, too. A great wooden beam split the ceiling; the rest of the room was of plaster. The room was very old, with rugs and jars and a few ancient chairs; the beam had once been the broken mast of a ship.

The captain of the ship had burned his wife's name into the mast and floated it home as a token of love; now it supported the house. Sotiris, looking, saw Dania walk into the room, and he knocked on the window. She turned; he signed to her to come out, and after kissing him, smiling, through the window, she walked carefully out so as not to awaken Mehmet Effendi.

"Agápimou," she said, "I hoped you would come."

"How are you?" asked Sotiris, wishing that he had not knocked.

"I'm well," she said. "I am so glad you came."

Once she had said to him, the first time, when he had asked her how she felt and asked her to be happy: "I love you very much, and that makes me very happy." And, much later, angry to feel her dependent, angry to feel himself caught, he had reminded her, smiling, that she had said "I love you" first. "I need no reminder," she said.

"I saw my grandmother today, took her to Charaki, all alone."

He looked at her wearing the white dress she wore, knew it was for him.

"And how is she?"

Once she had said to him, crying: "I feel sorry for a hairpin on the floor, that it should be alone."

"All right," Sotiris said. "She could be worse. She was contented to be home."

He watched the length of Dania's legs and the rise of her breasts and the long, full lightness of her hair. He looked at the depth of her eyes and the straightness of her nose and the little imperfection of her mouth.

"She promised me her money," he said.

Once Dania announced: "I feel sorry for you—I, without family," and it had angered him.

But now she said: "Sotis, that's wonderful. Tell me what happened," and they kissed.

He thought to himself: "She does not understand," and felt dominated again, by her submission. But he had heard the cat's noise in her throat when they kissed. He thought about her moments of abandon; he thought about the moment of her love.

Mehmet Effendi stirred; a cat behind them cried. Feeling her give herself up, he drew away, saying: "I'll tell you. But let's walk."

Alexis Saranditis had died in Scotland when Dania was ten. He had been on a pilgrimage and concert tour, reburying his wife. A year before, he had discovered, in a book, a letter written to him by his long-dead wife, Theon, asking him to bury her at home. As he was drunk, he promised her, holding the letter high, that he would take her back. As home was Lockerbie, a village in Scotland, where Theon had been born and lived her first five years, Alexis had much work to bear her ashes back. Her family was Greek, but they had come to Scotland as weavers in a mill, and only when the young Theon had started in to school, when she started to lose her Greek and speak to them as the Scottish people spoke, had they returned to Rhodes. She had been happy in Rhodes, had never more returned to Lockerbie, and just a girl cousin lived there. But Theon, in her letter, asked to be taken back, and, accordingly, Alexis set off. He had arranged a concert tour of France, and would also play in Manchester, but he flew first to Glasgow, where the girl cousin, unmarried still, and fat, drove up to meet him with his cello and his jug, two suitcases and no coat; he had not thought of rain.

But in Glasgow it rained: it rained the long drive down to Lockerbie, and all the rocks seemed rain. Alexis liked her fat; she drove with muscled legs, pumping at the clutch, and spoke Greek like a Turk; they stopped to have a drink. He said: "Theon would often speak of you." She laughed. "Yes, I expect so, saying naughty things." They drove up to her house; he set his cello on the floor and Theon's ashes on the table, went back to the car for his suitcases, and was killed. Opening the car door, in the thick yellow mist, he did not see the yellow light of an oncoming car and stepped straight out before it, was swept across the road. When Theon's cousin, holding drinks, came out to look for him, he lay there, in the mud, crumpled across his suitcase like a sheep, with hair stiff from the rain.

Her letter to Dania had been in broken Greek; Dania would not believe that her father was dead. Time passed; she only knew it when the lawyers came, appointing her sole heir, letting her keep the house, and telling her to have no further fear at all.

They walked out of the courtyard, down the street, and then stopped. Three little girls, about six years old, in red skirts and white blouses, jitterbugged in front of them. They had brought a black shell phonograph out in front

of their house, and they played on it, again and again, an
Italian rock-and-roll song, full of guitars and drums. The
guitars and drums brought Dania to a stop, and she smiled
at Sotiris and asked him to dance. She was an excellent
dancer and would often break out into dance when she and
Sotiris went walking; now, she jitterbugged to the Italian
music, making the children her partners. Sotiris stood and
watched, angry at her for not wanting to know what had
happened, excited to look at her dance.

The little girls, Dania's friends, were very happy and
danced with her, singing, until the end of the record, and
then again, singing the chorus, but when they started to
play the record for the third time, when her skirt had ridden up across her thighs, Sotiris took Dania by the hand
and walked her away from the girls.

"I'm sorry," she said. "I really want to hear. Tell me
about your day."

She held to him as they walked. He told her of his day.
When he had finished, she asked: "And what do you think
will happen?"

"I don't know," he answered, hurting her. "I just don't
know."

She was silent, thinking, but offered him her hand. He
looked at the lift of her breasts.

They walked under gables of houses, past windows of
white rooms where old women sat, until they were out into
widening streets, the long, tree-shaded streets of Monte
Smith. Coming down again out to the sea, on the far side
of the island, they walked to a tavérna and ordered a bottle
of wine. Sotiris thought of the two times he had drunk

with her, how she had grown drunk on only one bottle of wine and careened around the room, singing, hiccuping, dancing, asking him never to leave her, begging, and then being sick.

"I hope that everything will be all right," she said at last. "I hope your father won't be hurt."

The sea was in front of them, and the sunset, behind. Behind, a jukebox played, a drunk sang, and the proprietor of the tavérna argued with the drunk. Sotiris wanted her, now, for the way the men looked at her. So he finished his wine quickly, paid, and they went down the long sea road to the sea.

A wooden dock jutted into the sea, its planks twisted by rain. Sotiris, walking near to the side, felt, as he always did, the fear of the driving wind; he wondered if, falling, he should try to enter the water with head or feet first, or if there were large rocks below, and he thought of his body breaking open on the rocks.

"It's so quiet down here," she said, and he looked at her, wondering.

Near the end of the dock, a black lump of man turned to watch them, and Sotiris prepared himself, tense. But the man turned away, put together his tackle, and stood up with slung fish that slapped at his knees. Sotiris and Dania continued walking as the fisherman came past, with a rope around his belt slipped through the gills of his catch of coloured weakfish; they came to the end of the dock, and sat for a long time with their feet up on the boards, not speaking, with their arms around each other, and their bodies touching. He dropped his hand to her breast. He listened to the water and tried, as he always did, to separate the deep sound of water on the beach from the swirling of water on the soft dock legs. Distracted, he wished then that he were alone; Dania, hearing gulls, put her head on his shoulder.

"Come along, then," said Sotiris, kissing her.

They got up slowly, stretching, and he guided her onto the beach, down to black water and a little, abandoned black boathouse, with stone walls and boards for the windows. Now the tide was low, but waves were still high and loud upon the beach; they stood in front of the waves, on the hard, wet sand in front of the sea. He looked at the boathouse and saw they were truly protected, that he could not see the hospital lights, and that there was a little wooden ledge in front of the boathouse, three feet above the sand, built wide enough for a mattress and lying in sun, or for a surface to spread out the fish.

She fell on his neck and kissed him.

"**I**, THE YOUNGEST," Manos foretold, "shall earn no foot of land. Watch, just watch," he said, "possessionless, no feet."

Because of the street lights he could not see stars. Dressed again, walking with her back up the beach and dark hills of the New Town, taking her hand, tired of her, he said that he had to be home early in order to give them the news of his day.

The sun had set, and, above them, hospital lights glimmered in the pines of Monte Smith. He could not easily see her, and wished to himself he were gone. He could think of no reason to stay. But, in her street, in the half-light from the moon, he saw the three girls jitterbugging still to their never-ending song of "O mio bel amore." Seeing them, Sotiris felt a great returning rush of love, and he kissed Dania gently, saying: "Good night, agápi-mou."

Now the children noticed and came running, circling around them and dancing, making a ring with their hands, excited to play the game again, but Sotiris told them that he had to go, that they should also leave.

They ran away, singing, back to their song, and he turned back to Dania. Lying, he said: "Perhaps I'll return."

And when he turned to wave to her, she was standing still, in front of her doorway, watching him. He almost ran back to say that he loved and loved and loved her, but he did not, and he turned, followed by a great grey cat, to walk again out of the street.

Up the wind-swept hill, he looked in open windows, seeing white rooms and old people sitting. He turned to the right, away from the Turkish quarter and the mosques, until he came to a long wide courtyard bordered by peach and by pear and by tangerine trees. There, in the sweet-smelling darkness, under the walls of the Fort of the Crusaders, some couples stood kissing, tourists still walked, and a blind man sold mementos and sweetmeats by the wall. In the day, all the year, the blind man moved in sun like a puppet on string, but the castle wall and the tangerine trees shut sun out early, and he had been sitting for hours already in darkness, which was for him not the darkness but cold.

Sotiris waited until no one was watching. Then he walked past the blind man and climbed some stone steps on the wall of the courtyard; he stood, protected, hidden,

on the top of the wall, in a corner. Twenty-five feet down
the other side of the wall, oleander and bushes of bright
bougainvillea, mimosa bushes grew. Sotiris, sitting under
pear trees in a parapet of the wall, looked down to the
darkness that once was a moat and thought about Chrysanthi coming naked from the water.

In her room, Dania Saranditis was crying. She had seen
the old man to bed and had closed up the house, and now
she lay crying, obscurely, crying for the fact that Sotiris,
with his new-won money, would not want her any longer,
that he had loved her like a stranger, that she had loved
him back, crying for the fact of his going. She was not
weak, and she was proud, and she would not let him love
her like a stranger or a whore, and she said to herself that
she would leave him if he did not soon learn how to love.
Softly, so as not to awaken Mehmet Effendi, so as to hear
Sotiris if he should return, she lay crying on her bed,
wanting him, crying, telling herself it was only that he was
worried for his grandmother, watching the moon take the
colour from her room.

He stood on the stone wall, in front of the stone parapet, and watched the stars and spotlights play over his head
to the castle, for the Sound and Light Festival was started
now. He could hear the loud-speaker, behind him, blaring
the history of Rhodes loudly out over his head, first in
English, then in French, then, finally, in Greek.

"And so the statue of the Sun-God was raised from the

rubble of the siege of Demetrius Polyorcites, a siege as
colossal as the Colossus itself, and it was to commemorate
the peaceful ending of the great siege that Chares of
Lindos, spending the allotted three hundred talents and
working, in complete secrecy, for twelve long years, built
the hundred-foot prodigy, the wonder of the ancient
Aegean. . . ."

He thought about his grandmother, her poor, protected
house, and ninety-seven days.

The wind blew the loud-speaker sounds away, and he
heard the blind man then:

"Baklavádes and chocolates, loukoumádes, pine nuts;
buy from the blind."

"For fifty-six years until the earthquake of 227 B.C. sent
it toppling destroyed, the Colossus commanded the entrance to our harbour, the very harbour behind us, now
named Mandraki, where, walking, you might well see a
Greek boy looking like that ancient Greek whose image
Chares of Lindos captured in metal."

Sotiris, full with wine and aching with having made
love, unzipped his pants, and, turning carefully out toward the bougainvillea, relieved himself onto the wall,
staining the darkness of stone.

He thought about Dania, and leaving her alone.

"Nougats, almonds, baklavádes, galatoboúrika, and pine
nuts; buy mementos from the blind."

"I don't want to walk any more," said a man holding a
woman close in the courtyard. "Let's go back to the room."

"For nine hundred years, then, the Sun-God lay shattered in front of the town, a grim reminder of the earth-

quake that had toppled it, until, in the seventh century
A.D., a Jew from Syria bought the twisted metal scraps and
packed them onto camels. . . ."

"All right," she said.

"Baklavádes and chocolates, loukoumádes, pine nuts."

"I need you," said the woman.

"The legend says that it took nine hundred camels to
transport the body of the statue back to Syria, and there
the Jew boiled all the fragments down and sold them again
for great profit."

"Galatoboúrika and pine nuts; buy mementos from the
blind."

"I need you so very much."

"He must have done a thorough job, for no attempts to
locate further fragments of the lost Colossus have suc-
ceeded. Archaeologists, treasure-hunters, curiosity-seekers
of all kinds and from all nations have dug and dug and
have found nothing. Every few years, however, a new team
dredges the bottom of the harbour of Mandraki, and it
remains yet to be seen whether something may be found."

He thought about Syria, deserts and seas; he thought
about Athens and a far country.

"Come quickly, then," said the man.

Sotiris climbed down the steps of the wall and started
to walk to his home.

Dania Saranditis lay in her bed, thinking: "He said he
might come back."

THE PROCOPIRIOS HOUSE is large, of yellow cement, on the hill that slopes down to Mandraki. It is one of the largest houses in the New Town, for Apelis, well-born and well-married, is rich. On the first floor are the kitchens and the pantry, always full, for Apelis sometimes trades rough cloth to the peasants, who bring him new partridge and bushels of fruit and fresh squid in exchange. The living rooms and dining room lie also on the first floor; the second floor holds five bedrooms, and the third floor as many again—four for the servants, and one, by his choice, for Sotiris.

Having looked out the window to see that nobody could hear, Andreas Procopirios turned, in his father's house, to his wife, Aliki, saying: "You are sure?"

"Yes."

"Well, then, how do you know?"

"I feel it," she answered.

"What does that mean, you feel it?"

"It means that I know."

Outside, a dog barked. She turned to him, speaking more softly: "Darling, oh what shall we do?"

"Don't call me darling," he wanted to say.

She waited, her lower lip trembling. He looked at her, thinking her ugly. He looked at the window and out at the moon-coloured sky. "Don't cry now, at least, please," he wanted to say.

"Is it because it will anger your father?"

"That doesn't," he lied, "worry me."

"Because I told you in his house?"

"You could have waited, yes."

"But what is so terrible?" All at once strident, she asked him, "Well, don't you think he'll be glad?"

"Yes," Andreas said. "What made you tell me here?"

"Well, we can afford it, and don't you want children?"

Andreas answered yes.

"Koúklamou, thank you." She threw her arms round him and laughed.

In the rear of the house, facing away from the street, bounded by a high cement wall and by vines, stretched a stone patio. Yannis, the drunk, cousin to dead Nicoletta, lay sprawled on a table, half-sleeping. A dog barked; he awoke. Andreas and Aliki were inside. Yannis popped open a bottle of beer and the foam from it spilled to the table; laughing, he called to Apelis to come and to join in the drink.

"Yes, yes, in a minute," answered Apelis, standing alone by the wall.

"Drunkard," he thought to himself. "Go 'cut the ripe figs,' as you call it, with village girls in the fields. I wait for my son to return."

Sotiris walked home through a gate leading out to the sea. A long row of women with lanterns stood lined upon the road above the beach, and there, past the harbour, on a little shelf of sand, fishermen dragged in a net. They moved with swollen feet full of salt water, and there, in the moon, the cords of their arms were like cords of the net as they pulled at the weight of the catch.

He regretted his promise now not to go searching, for he would feel hunted when everyone knew. Everyone would be watching him always, wondering whether he too had been tricked. And there would be insults, jokes, admiration: he wished it did not have to be.

As the fishermen pulled, the sound of fish slapping at each other grew louder than the sound of waves. Separating the kalamarákia, the small squid, from the frantic red mullet, keeping both, the men threw the useless and tasteless fish back to the sea. The waiting women climbed down then to look at the catch, shining their lanterns on buckets, sifting the not-yet-dead fish and arguing over their price. Sotiris walked on.

Inside the garden, he saw his father and said: "Yásou, papa."

"Ya, Sotiris," said Apelis, coming near. "You are late."

"Forgive me, I have eaten," lied Sotiris. "And you?"

He wondered if his father had been told.

"Ya, Sotis," cried a man in shadow, throwing back his

head. "Come here, drink, come and tell us what happened. We have been waiting so long."

He recognized Yannis sitting at the table, and knew then that he would have found out and told, would have asked at the hospital after Orsetta, to find she had gone, at the least.

"How is Orsetta, Sotiris?"

"Yes, let us talk," said his father. "Alone. I want to hear what has happened."

He knew that his father expected the treasure himself.

"We'll go over there, and we'll talk," said Apelis, pointing to a fig tree by the wall.

Yannis turned back to his drink.

"All right," said Apelis, now standing in darkness.

Sotiris looked back at the house.

Once, he remembered, at the very end of the war, when he was still a very small boy, his father had taken Andreas and him for a walk. They had gone to the hills, to a grove of fig trees, down a ditch, through a hole in the hill, into a cave full of boxes and guns.

"How is your grandmother?"

All the long night he had waited for this, and now it would have to be told.

"I said, how is your grandmother, boy?"

He looked at his father and thought to himself: "All right, how?"

"Where is your tongue?" asked Apelis, impatient. "I asked you a question, or do you not hear any more?"

Sotiris looked down at the pattern of stone, saying: "Endáxi, she is well. I found her very well."

"What do you mean by that—well?"

"She is in Charaki," said Sotiris, knowing that his father knew so, too.

"Charaki?"

"Yes. I went with her there, today. She wanted very much to go, she asked particularly, and the doctors agreed."

The cave was big and dark; he had been proud and afraid. In the cave, quietly, Apelis had told them; Sotiris remembered how his father had nodded when he told them that if ever they needed him at home, and he was gone for very long, they could look for him there. His father had stood in the dark.

"She is all right," said Sotiris. "The trip did not hurt her at all."

Moonlight through fig leaves dappled his father's face, spattering hands.

"Does she want to stay there?" asked Apelis.

The leaves of the fig tree were white.

"I don't know."

"Well then, what do the doctors say?"

"I don't know. I'm sorry. They all gave their consent."

"Is anyone with her?"

"Anna-Maria, of course."

"Is that all?" asked Apelis.

"Yes."

"No nurse, no attendant. Nobody at all?"

The cave had seemed empty. But, when he was older, after the war, after his father had gotten a medal for leading guerrilla resistance, he had often returned. Sometimes, dreaming, under the hill full of trees, he discovered an old can of food or a knife.

The moon made his father's face white.

"For my lack of care," Sotiris said, "I am sorry. I was wrong. Please forgive."

A dog barked. Over the wall, he could hear the cicadas. Apelis asked suddenly: "Why did she go?"

"To give me the treasure!" he wanted to say. He looked at the wall and the sky.

"Why did she go?" asked Apelis again.

"To show me the money," he said.

"Did she?"

"Yes," said Sotiris. "She showed where it was. She gave it to me."

He had tried to be his father, sitting on a stone by the entrance to the ditch, dreaming, awaiting Italians, practising slow speech.

But now he repeated: "She gave all of it to me."

"Fifty-seven, fifty-eight," and Apelis stopped. Sotiris, eleven, tired, held his legs. His father exercised each morning, and Sotiris always watched, helping if he could. Today he held his father's legs while Apelis sat up, stretching his arms and touching hand to toe. His father's sweat wet through the exercising pants and soaked Sotiris' hand; he yawned, the smell was very strong. And, sometimes, at the end, Apelis and he would box. "Fifty-nine," Apelis said, and turned onto his side.

He had expected his father angry or hurt; one or the

other, not silent. So now he stared, without reaction, at the little lines upon his father's neck and chin and wondered what else he could say, wondered if it was done.

"Why didn't you bring it home?" asked Apelis. "If it is yours, as you say."

"Because," he explained, "she would not let me search for it—not until she dies. She wanted to keep it till then, and, equally, I have to wait."

Apelis Procopirios put his hand to his mouth and rubbed along the muscles of the jaw. He looked at the yellow walls of his house, at the sky, at Sotiris, his second son, whom he loved above all, but without forgiveness, and said: "Now listen to me, will you please."

A plane overhead turned to land.

"You know, do you not," said Apelis, "that I was already alive when Italians drove Turks from the island and governed the Greeks in their place. There always was someone to govern the Greeks. So that, as I grew, I watched the Italians with their guns and ships, the governor sometimes in a car, until I went to work for Italians building the forum down in Mandraki. 'Foro Italico,' they called it then."

"Why does he tell me this?" wondered Sotiris, who, indeed, did know.

"Foro Italico, si. And it was Mario, the one-legged mason I worked with, who taught me Italian and told me to go to America. Every day, eating lunch on a stone in the harbour—myself on the lower stone, listening—one-legged Mario spoke of America, cars and high houses, of President Wilson who saved the whole world."

"I have no wish to go to America."

"No—perhaps not. But to travel and dream, to be free! That is another thing, and what I have not told you is that, because of his lies, I set off. Vláhos! I went, dreaming of President Wilson and gold, getting there in 1931, finding neither. I was twenty-three, and, vláhos, on a stupid treasure hunt! I found neither one nor the other—and you, little Sotis, twenty, are on one already. No! No!" He was excited now, using his hands. "Don't interrupt me—listen until I have finished for once. You know, I have told you, I'll take Andreas into the business, have already done so, but for you there will be something better—government, perhaps, or finance. Not your songs. And you will never be a diplomat or banker, no, not even a man, if you believe an old lying woman who tells you her money is yours but will not offer proof. She has fooled Manos and Triphon once, too."

"I believe her," said Sotiris, and asked himself whether he did. "I am not a diplomat or banker, who cannot believe without proof."

"Believe her, believe, but how can you believe when the money will surely be mine? Sotis, you're a good boy, a well-meaning boy, but no businessman. And where do you think you'd be now if I had believed in what everyone promised? In this house, in these clothes? No, not at all. No, no, it is mine, and you should not be disappointed."

"She gave it to me," repeated Sotiris. "Every last drachma is mine."

"But how could she do that? She must have been teasing you, can you not see?" And pushing his head for-

ward and down, in the crowding, close way that he had as a
boxer and used, still, when working a bargain, Apelis said:
"Tell me what happened, exactly."

Looking at the fig tree, the fistfuls of wood, Sotiris told
his father, carefully, what had happened, leaving out only
the name of the place where Orsetta Procopirios had
pointed and ordered him to look. Then Apelis challenged
him, saying: "Take it, if you can get to it, boy, even the
part that is mine. I offer everything to you, on the condition only that you obey and do not go back to search until
she dies. So that, if you trust in my mother, therefore, and
find the money because of your trust, it is yours. If it is
lost, it is lost. Unless, of course," and he smiled, "she gives
it away, in the meantime, to me. That is the lesson I'll
teach. If you are wrong and should not have believed her,
it will stay lost or be mine."

And Sotiris answered: "Agreed."

A boat from Crete
not big, nor small
but fifty cubits long
casts anchor
here at Rhodes.
The men go to the sea.
I too, I, too,
go down to see
to visit her I love
and ask her for a kiss.
She asks me for money.

> *"And where am I to find money,*
> *I, a wanderer?*
> *I go together with the ships*
> *and I have no money."*

Tired, leaving his father, he went from the garden and house, not wanting to go to his room, and walked down the hill to Mandraki. Mandraki, the main harbour of Rhodes, held the flat, snout-nosed island caïques, the blue and white sleek sporting yachts, and that night it held the cruise ships from Venice and Athens and Dubrövnik. At the bottom of the harbour, yachts and island caïques and Italian warships lay together, wrecked. The water of the harbour, even at midnight, was blue and clear and beautiful; Sotiris stood by the water and thought about going away. "Please stay," Dania had asked, and Orsetta also. The coloured strings of lights upon the cruise ships, the lights in the rigging of yachts, and the lanterns on the snouts of the red and blue caïques dotted the water like confetti, and the lights moved on the water like confetti in the wind.

Tangerine trees spattered the walls of the harbour in groves. As a child, Sotiris had often climbed up their trunks to pick tangerines; frightened, free, he had pretended to be a muezzin who sang out of stone minarets. Sometimes, when he had felt wild enough and the sea had been near enough, he had left his clothes at the bottom of the wall, had climbed the tree naked to drop down ripe fruit, had jumped reaching after it into the sea.

Now, singing his noiseless song, he walked down the

flagstone and tar piazza that ran the length of Mandraki. To the left of the piazza rose the old walled city; on the right, up into Monte Smith, rose the white plaster walls and red roofs of the New Town. There was a great open market set back from the piazza, where, in the morning, all the nearby farmers and artisans would come to sell, and all the women come to buy. Then the market would be the center of the twin cities of Rhodes, full of the noises of selling and buying; it would be full of whole hanging lambs and bushels of grapes and olives and figs, full of the flowers and fruits and the fish, barrels of wine and jars and woven baskets, and the strong, fresh smell of food.

But Sotiris stood alone in the stone entrance gate, for until the early morning, when the fishermen and farmers would come to put their stalls together, the market would stay empty and clean. Looking, Sotiris saw that the first delivery of watermelon had arrived, that the great green karpoúzia were stacked against a wall, behind a row of hand carts, high into the air. Then he saw rinds and seeds scattered all over and littering ground. Disgusted, he thought of the men who had gorged on the karpoúzia, sating themselves, until, looking again at the pile by the wall, he saw himself eating through all of the melons, looking for treasure, swimming in watermelon heart, filling his belly with husks and with rind, spitting out black seeds that rattled and jingled and clanked as they fell.

Apelis, standing in the shadow of the fig tree, saw

Yannis sprawled on the table and went to wake him. The drunk.

Sotiris had gone to the house. He had said: "I believe her," convinced. Well, she had fooled Manos and Triphon once, too, using his money. Awake.

America, he said to himself, only why? Why, speaking of it, did he stop—and, vláhos, finish up saying nothing at all? America—why had he stopped, just then, with Sotiris, just when he started to tell? And Sotiris knew some of the facts: that he had worked in a steel mill, losing the job when the mill had closed down; that he lost his job in the Pittsburgh garment factory, when the factory, laying off non-Americans first, went to half-time—he could speak of all that easily enough, but it had not been important, was not what America meant.

The hovels near Pittsburgh where men with no work lived, some of them dying; the little-known language; begging and bread lines; big-bellied children, some of them his, perhaps; proud letters home that had lied about money and told them how well he was; weakness and fear —why had he not revealed that? In the mockery of Orsetta's one visit, he tricked her to think of him well. He had never told anyone; nobody knew; not even Nicoletta, when they were married, and he had tried hard to forget. She had not made it easy, his poor Nicoletta, approaching him but as a priest, obeying unspoken commands. How humble one's self to one's slave? Apelis crushed leaf against leaf.

And those things would be easier still to tell to his son

than the rest; what he tried now never to remember and could not forget, what he lay sweating next to at night— the way he had finally grown rich, and what it had done to his pride. Black-marketing, house-cleaning, dish-washing, dog-walking, all he had done for the rich. The servants in his father's house, he had told himself then, were better provided than he.

Apelis took hold of the drunken man's arm.

"Éla! Take care!" protested the shaken Yannis.

"Then wake up!" he answered. "Go off to your own house for sleeping, if you are tired."

"Tired? Why tired? From what?" asked Yannis. "From digging in the earth, or in a girl? You can find treasure in both, in the center, eh? Near to the bowels in both."

Apelis answered yes.

A strong wind was blowing. Sotiris walked down the sea road to the sea and to the little black boathouse where he had last been with Dania. Shadowed from the hospital lights and the lights of the New Town, he took off his clothes quickly, laid them on the ledge, walked into wind, and then stood in front of the sea.

Childless, Signor Smith spawns oleander leaves, and they point to the country he left. "May your juice be as bitter," he said, "as homecoming has been to me."

The water was warmer than air; the waves pulled and slapped; Sotiris could see purple and white fish below. Diving down, he saw phosphore on his body sending long sparks to the sand, and he wheeled around and around in the water, watching the phosphore spark and circle, frightening the fish. Then he swam back to the shore, rubbed himself down with his hands, and, dressed, his skin still feeling slimy from the phosphore, he walked up the beach and the hills.

Beside him, the Englishman wept.

Underneath the mosque, near Dania's house, he stretched out to sleep, and he lay there, staring at the sky and the dawn winds in trees until he fell asleep. At five, Sotiris was wakened by the cry of cats and the call of the muezzin, and he left, thinking: "I cannot stay."

PART TWO

aTHens

A PARALLELOGRAM disjointed with the warp, the parallels become an arch and fallen in to hold, Sotiris saw the chair, blue paint unapplied underneath, a coil of leather thong to bolster sagging straw, the wood wormholed and splintering, all logical, in rows, the plaited seat unsafe, two cross beams for the front legs where hung his sleeping hand, ornate carved monkey cracked, but one remaining dowel for the sides and rear, black rims in six forsaken slots, and hair, above the arching seat a bent back-rest unstuck—above the empty, honeycomb-shaped straw, hive-holding leather strap, lap distance from the chair, he saw the table bottom, oil stains spreading D, saw blue paint peeled upon his great abandoned height. He rubbed his back on floor; he touched the chair's four feet. He went back to the bed.

Sotiris lay alone: two faces and a reaching hand had welcomed him within. These people wait for me, he said, and pushed aside the door. Chrysanthi waits attained—

each single thing unchanged. To find them grinning tooth-lessly, at his recovered bed, to terrify them in return with a cut dog-shark's eye—he entered, posturing. And yet a great way off, he watched them wearing cloaks. Its black blinded expanse twice as large as his mouth, and all the white supporting flesh still wetted down with ice, he held, cylindrical, his eye, the retina unrimmed and soft, flesh shredding at the sides, a bit of paper bag embedded by an edge—he watched them blink and blink.

The memory is clear, he said, and prodded them with picks. Fish tastes best at the bone, white ligament dissolved (he saw the table bottom, oil stains spreading D, trans-lucent now, above him, framed in straw). There is no thing more purposeless, time past, than meat that still cleaves to the bone. He stretched his neck to laugh; he stroked the dog-shark eye. Inordinate, your bone, the single support of your high vanished back. What shall I say, how best explain my coming, now that I, again, am here? To offer you my house. The brown sticking paper flaked onto his wrist; beneath the swollen retina, thin blood cascaded down. And all for dissection, at last; to hold your sleeping hand.

The waste of what remained, the little substance left, possessed him wholly now; he turned upon his side.

Inside his shop, alone, Apelis tried to count the racks. Starting from the floor, moving just his head, he numbered fabrics up to the ceiling, but three times lost count near the top, and, angry, had to start again.

What more to prepare for the party tomorrow; what of

the treasure, Andreas, Orsetta, himself? Apelis' eye, this fourth time, strayed, the green grew confused with the blue, thirteen was fourteen perhaps, and the task without point. All of his thoughts were away.

Where was Sotiris? Why had he gone? What of police? Was he safe?

Apelis pulled the shutters to, locked doors behind, and left.

Three-legged, a brown dog limped toward a newspaper, turned it over, fell. A waiter laughed and laughed. Sotiris turned to face the wall.

"Aphrodite, born of pain, place a garland on her neck, cover it with spray."

Suddenly a son again, he lay upon his back, upon a cliff, in memory, hearing cicadas and bees.

Long grass blanketed his leg; he drank warm milk from a gourd. Olive trees upheld the sky.

"Stream the blood upon her hair; hammer down the hand."

Awakening, one morning, in his room, Sotiris found Orsetta's money spent, every drachma gone, her six bedraggled treasures, and his last restraint.

Carefully, Merope, hare-lipped, seventeen, pencilled beard and moustache on the women of a calendar. "Ouzo," said Yerassimos. And, "Éla! Come along!" the waiter called, summoning the dog, holding out his empty hand, a broom behind his back.

Like water rippling round a stick, the city spread below: a history of change.

"A chicken with no head is love, an iceberg without
base." A sad stone mason carved the heads of saints.

Sotiris' room was long, white-walled and low, with beams
for the ceiling and white-painted wood for the floor; over
his bed, the ceiling swooped down. He had lived in the
room for three months. His bed, too, was long, white and
low, iron-framed. The windows had been poorly fitted
and stood angular, askew, with cracks in the plaster that
made the wind sing.

"Chrýsomou, my golden one, only come answer me
this. . . ."

Within unseeing eyes, the mason circled life; upon a
folded hand he ordained thorns. "No quickness left," he
said, "to finger any chord. Work ruins all my play; don't
ever carve for fun."

A single string, unravelled, circled the bouzoúki neck
and trailed to lemon oil; Sotiris tore it back.

Below him lived a widow and sister, a shoemaker, idiot,
café waitress. The idiot, he could hear, was wheeling his
pushcart in front of the house, filling it full with pistachio
nuts, preparing to sit the day through.

"One hand grown thick with hammering, and the other,
blunt. Nobody listens now."

Blue langouste and a dead fish head together in a tank,
scales trailing decomposed, fresh-water pond he pictured
eight miles from the sea, littered with donkey leavings and
the tall marsh birds, a ruin, absolute. ("I'll make myself

a mandolin, with Nicaraguan ebony wood, then take it to Peru.") "Alluvial, I shall deposit this," Sotiris heard, and could not feel his arm. "Chrysanthi, I could go."

He shifted the sheets; it was bravado; he knew he could not leave. He had arrived three months before, flying down from Cape Sounion to land—and nothing was decided yet, nothing was made clear.

Yorgo, the idiot, sang to himself a wet singsong, tuneless, without end. He straightened the nuts, placed them in piles, both his feet beat time. It was early morning now; the sun could reach his neck. Christoforos, cobbler, went to work again, considering the army boots desired by a count; they stood upon his working bench, never finished, never bought. The sun that woke him to his job allowed Katina sleep; she had come home at five. Thetis and Theoni, widow and sister, wondered if she lay alone. Sotiris, at the top, had his recurrent dream.

Huddled, one hand across his face, he dreamt again of Rhodes:

A phonograph ticked time. A bayonet became a snake. There were rows of jars. It was a shop, and he the customer; his donkey lay outside. Mehmet Effendi, salesman, laughed. In the field a cat was tied, mouth open to a tap, with water ballooning the cat's belly out till it burst. In the shop again, bargaining how deep to dig, an ear of corn grew from the slime; he slipped the knife, the bayonet, beneath his shirt and ran. Mehmet Effendi laughed, brandishing the cat. Now, running, he began to bleed; it was a snake and would not die; long tree-lined streets toward the sea; the donkey had been wounded, too; it was a cave he dug, a grave, a cave, Chrysanthi cried and cried. "Where have you been?" he asked, adoring. "Chrýsomou, where have you been?"

When he awakened, she stood in the room. Black sand slipped over his bayonet blade. He struggled to tell her "Hello."

"You were asleep," Chrysanthi said, and bent to stroke the cat.

When she entered, a challenge, pitting her beauty with his, saying, "Well, at the least, I am back," it was as when, three months before, he had recognized her first—alive again, returned.

IMPATIENT, flowing, far ahead, Andreas turned his head to call: "Come along, Sotiris, we cannot always wait!" Bodies riding smoothly with the rhythm of a canter, Andreas and his friend had horses now; Sotiris, eight, was still too young. Still upon his donkey, bounced and jiggled by the trot, unable to force it into a canter, last, he saw the others fly across the field and knew he would be left.

The ambulance of Rhodes had once belonged to the French Consul. When, however, it served him no more as a Consulate car, when it was years old and of no further use as a private limousine, six years before, as an act of kindness, in a ceremony, the Consul had given it to the hospital—and now it was the ambulance.

The old black limousine had been repainted white: the rear seat, where once the Consul's son would lie with the easy and frightened Greek village girls on nights when the moon split the sea, had been replaced by two metal beds. It was a standing joke among the people at the Consulate that the car looked more of a hearse than an ambulance, for the paint had flaked to an uneven grey.

The Consul, when whirling some white-faced and half-hearing visitor on a tour of Rhodes, would never fail to say, as his new sleek car passed the old one, that the Mission of Mercy is slow. Then he would tell the little story of his gift, while the overtaken ambulance blew a token of respect, and the visitor sat smiling sleepy-eyed with one hand in the window strap and one hand on the seat.

Mehmet Effendi, walking near the hospital, saw the ambulance, its windows glittering in sun. Pomegranate trees stabbed the yellow walls to scarlet; pink and white oleander bushes, beautiful and poison-juiced, crowded to the gate. He stood, unsure, at the head of the arched and gravel driveway, but chose not to speak to the ambulance driver, to tell him nothing and no more.

Hunchbacked, an old woman walked with a cretin, jibbering softly and making him laugh. Flagstones spread upon the courts, cobbles on the alleyway, paving on the street.

"Will you come to Rhodes with me?"

"Why?" She took it as a joke.

"Because I will return soon, and want to be with you."

"Then stay a little longer, here."

"I should go back."

Chrysanthi said: "Then go."

He had been with her three months, had seen her first

by chance. Lonely one late afternoon, and nearing a theatre, he had gone inside.

Men with packages, cars, children filled the street.

Yorgo, the idiot, attentive now, prepared his paper bags.
Mouth open, smooth, he lined them up, then crumpled
them to start again.

The picture was American, a Western, with posters all
over the lobby, no more than a way to pass time. He
curled upon his seat to watch.

The workers in his father's field could sing like wind,
but moved like ants. He lay upon the cliff.

Men there came and called to friends, banging the green
wooden slats of their seats, loud as the noise of the film.
In the intermissions, while Sotiris sat, vendors came calling: "Loukomádes, halva, cold portokaláda."

"Ouzo," said Yerassimos.

The sea unfurled beneath.

Banging back chairs as they stood, then, beating a tattoo
of answering sound, the men arose and shouted for service,
gesticulated, some of them rolling their emptied bottles of
beer and fruit drink, portokaláda, down the slanted floor.

Many-coloured coats the city wore—many-coloured
stone.

In the second intermission, there, in the noise of buying and selling, Sotiris had turned to see a woman stand,
black against the lobby lights, then move, escorted by men.

The bed, two chairs, and a table with washstand were
the only furniture; he lay at the top of the house.

Athens anticipated day with surge of workers into work,
of sun along the street.

And when, at last, the group chose seats two rows in

front of him, when she turned round to royally look at the people behind, he, the light full on her face, recognized Chrysanthi.

"Were you alone?" she asked. "What did you do last night?"

The three men with her took their seats, all disturbance passed. But he could neither move nor speak, and soon she turned again to sit, banging down the wooden slats, taking his stomach away.

Christoforos, cobbler, locked the door. Then, slowly, reverent, he turned toward his riding boots and pulled them on, walked in secret circles round the room, listening for customers, a piece of brown leather for whip.

Sotiris saw three yellow birds fly across his eyes. He closed his eyes again.

Two rows ahead, two seats across, placed so that he could only see her profile, and could not stay sure it was she, Chrysanthi sat, while silently he said her name, over and over, his blood pounding time.

"You should have come," Chrysanthi said. "I missed you very much."

He turned away from her, turned to face the wall.

"The others asked about you, why you hadn't come."

Once he had changed seats, trying to see her face. Beyond that, of the theatre, he remembered, noticed nothing —only the back and small left side of Chrysanthi's head.

Thetis and Theoni sat over breakfast, Thetis content, Theoni sad.

"Yellow birds of death," he said into the sheets, "blanket my horse—old song."

All he could afterwards remember was a scene in which the hero spied through a keyhole upon the beautiful and naked heroine bathing in a barrel. She, meeting his eye, and probably she knew he'd stare whenever she undressed, smiled, then threw a handful of suds at the door.

Today it was Theoni's turn to buy the luncheon meal.

He had laughed at the comic, surprised face of the man, withdrawing from the door, a keyhole shape of suds across his eye, and he remembered the long, naked girl in a barrel of soap.

"An old song. These are sheets."

"What did you do?" she asked.

"Blanket my horse, my horse."

How could he tell her he only had lain, wanting, awaiting her step?

She had turned toward him then.

Now she stroked the cat.

How could he tell her he wanted to go, now that she was come again?

"I missed you very much last night," Chrysanthi said and smiled.

He had whispered out her name, the time that she had turned.

"Chrýsomou," he whispered now. "Chryso, Chrýsomou."

Katina slept, one arm across her face to keep away the light, one hand between her thighs.

WHEN STAVROS collected his sheep, helped by the three sheep dogs, holding his crook and whistling, throwing stones to guide them after him, Valeria would come with no coaxing, stepping near to his hand. And when he milked the goats, keeping the lambs and kids at a distance so that they could not suck, Valeria would sidle near and stand watching with him, eating her barley cake or hay, her crushed oats, roots, and corn. He fed her maize and linseed cake, the best grass and whole milk. She lay down by his side.

But, four months old, at the start of the summer, she had grown suddenly sick. Stavros had noticed first how nervous she became, not eating, breathing quickly, coughing, spitting foam around her mouth, restless, switching her tail. And then, after the second day, he understood: she had eaten an apple or orange, had been unable to swallow or digest it, unable to disgorge or cough it back; all of her gasses had stayed in her stomach and, blocked, could not escape. She would soon choke with gas. Stavros

felt the fruit on the left side of her neck, massaged the
lump and fed her turpentine and oil, but the fruit stayed
fixed. Valeria grew very frightened, could not swallow
food or water, could not free her blocked throat. Gas
swelled in her stomach, distending the skin, expanding,
growing great. Behind the last rib, by the hip, bloated
with gas, the abdomen hung out, on the left side, swollen
and tight, a sack of poison, stiff. Stavros approached; she
kicked and tried to bellow, coughed. He held her tightly
to his hip, pulled back upon her nose and tried to force
the apple down, to clear away the throat, could not. He
used a stick, could not. His hand was wet with foam.
Valeria lay down to die; he could not do a thing. She lay
down on the ground, on her right side, the hillock of her
stomach rising high.

And finally, he took his knife, crossed and commended
himself, then closed his eyes and pierced her abdomen so
that it burst, a poison bubble, so that the gas escaped.
Writhing, and in her cry of pain, Valeria brought an entire apple out. And Stavros dressed her wound, massaged
the flank, and fed her water; soon, she stood again.

One of the men at the theatre, introduced outside,
seemed Sotiris himself. His twin brother, surprised, non-
existent but dreamed of, the prince of some far-distant
realm, elegantly dressed, his double, the bones in their
hand spread alike, his face in a mirror, stared back. That
man, Phillipos Stritsas, held Chrysanthi's arm.

Where they walked the flowers bent and rabbits followed hopping; rain had gathered in a barrel; warm, they stooped to drink. Rings whispered on her finger, robes upon her arm; the water spreading from her mouth lapped softly at the staves. Anemones and crocus, iris, almond flowers; a wreath of narcissi she wore, and offered him her hand. If anyone know all the truth, answer, he proclaimed: how bracelets bind my love.

An island called No-island stood four miles from the shore; the Air Force practised bombing it and shook their window frame. Sotiris plucked a branch. Am I kept by my brother, that need know where he lies? Look under great acacia trees if you desire gold.

The path was steep and rocky, with rivulets of sand; she slipped; he held her, laughing, righted her once more. An axe blade in the distance arced; he heard, delayed, the slap on wood. Metal rose to fall again a mountainside away.

A fire, finished, soaked to ash, had gutted all one house. Workers threw down lamp shades, rags of clothing, chairs. He watched possessions turn to waste, and what was cherished, scraps. Even a plaster bird was burned, and walls were barrel thin.

My father wants me endlessly to work within his mine. I till the ground and keep the sheep; I pipe his only tune. My brother is myself. I need no sermons, priest, but just your surgery. The king is very dead. And when kings die, quick, change their picture in the station house; put princes in their stead.

Next, madly singing by the sea, they came upon a Scotsman playing pipes, the bagpipes huge, belabored, his ankles in the surf and pants above the knee. Red hairs curled

from the Scotsman's calf, a white line showing waves. He
covered with a scarf her hand and shod her little foot.
Beneath the bagpipe trough and crest, he heard incoming
air. Forgive, Sotiris cried, the paste upon my hand. Put
hot cups where the cold may be, to draw away the pain.
And never sleep in shade. I pick a piece of marble up to
hold my quarried home.

Within the created expanse, no shelter but a stone, and
that, he dreamed, he ate.

"I will not pass again out through this narrow place."
Orsetta, on her bed, followed a dragonfly. It circled in her
house, a line of blue and black, and holding that good
news, she crossed herself and said: "Not ever through this
place. Barbarians, these people, never care. Someone," Orsetta thought, "has got three hairs from off my head, or
off my old clothing, strands from the carob chest, drives
nails into my stomach, is giving me this pain. Until Sotiris comes." She listened for his step. "Or scrapes me with
a knife, or puts me in a stream, so that I slowly wear
away." Pretending rest again, she turned her head to
watch.

Five years old, he watched the wall to see if it would
move with evening, saw his uncle smoke. "White maiden
with fair hair, white, white as milk," Manos intoned, "my
cigarettelet, kiss my lip." Sotiris asked for biscuits as a
proof of love. He ate them at one sitting, demanded proof
again. Uncle Manos told him daytime stories in the night:
"Your great-grandfather fought the Turks, and his father before him was a priest. Twelve children, however, he

had, six sons, all of them sailors, and just one returned. No longer with his legs. One, Turks had cut, the other he himself destroyed to leave it in a chain. Legless, he swam from the prisoner boat, and salt sea cured his wound. He pulled himself ashore, they say, and cried for forgiveness from sad stumps of knees. The famine ended then, and land around Malona was his hero's prize."

Manos, circling Sotis' eyes with wet forefinger, broken nail, would warn him to his upturned face that he, a Procopirios, had much to remember and learn.

In Athens, in three months, Sotiris learned of isolation, and he learned contempt.

PRETENDING to be an onshore guest come to say farewell to friends, giving himself a false name, Sotiris had walked to a tourist boat leaving the harbour of Rhodes. The boat, he discovered, took mainly English, Italian, and French passengers, was bound for Corfu, making a luxury tour of the islands, was to stop next at Syros. And, when the boat left, Sotiris left too.

For hours he had walked around the decks, speaking little, smiling at the passengers and crew, eating squid and chicken from the open buffet tables, choosing the best place to hide. Then, in the dark, with nobody watching, he climbed into a lifeboat and waited, curled beneath canvas, feeling the pitch of the sea. Half asleep, protected from wind, looking at the sky and strings of coloured lights, he listened to the motor and a midnight dance. A couple came and whispered in his ear; finally, he slept.

At dawn, he clambered out again and sat stiffly on the foredeck, hearing the first gulls come out to the ship, watching the cold sun come up on his left side, the moon going dim on the right.

In the early morning, then, the boat docked at Syros. When vendors below had crowded the gangplank, when a sweetmeat seller, in his excitement, had run all the way to the top, Sotiris, awaiting his chance, mixed with a large group of men and slipped past the ship's officers. At bottom, when he had walked fifty feet from the boat, someone called loudly: "Sir, M'sieur, Signore!" but he did not turn around.

Nor did he stay in Syros. Having bought a room and bath, he walked that afternoon to the beach and met there a pilot, watching the girls. The pilot was named Kimon, and many people knew him, bringing fish and beer with which to sit, or simply crying as they passed, "Ciao, Kimon," and "Yásou." Sotiris ate his lunch staring at the sea, but Kimon, alone for a moment, threw up his hands and called out: "Do you see the goddess?" When Sotiris had looked where he pointed and signified yes, Kimon continued: "Well, that is her mother"—pointing to a stern woman dressed still for town. "The old one, she knows I am married, and therefore I cannot approach." Then, smiling, he came and sat down.

("Fidelity," Sotiris thought. "A word that means nothing—correct, Chrýsomou? For what does it mean if not to stay faithful, and why not to more than one thing? If you are more than one yourself?")

Kimon worked as a fleet pilot, taking his plane across the islands, spotting the large schools of fish and then alerting the fleet. Some days, in accordance with the weather or his mood, he would not work at all; some days, using auxiliary tanks, he would spend twelve or thirteen hours nonstop in the air, and sometimes he spent six and six. Tomorrow, he said, he would leave at dawn, cover the waters, and land on the mainland for lunch; if Sotiris came, he could reach Athens by two.

Kimon's plane was an old, brown, English army training plane, with two seats, excellent dual controls, and radio. He had not asked Sotiris to pay for the trip: clearly he had wanted company, and all through the morning, as they swooped and circled, he spoke to Sotiris of the islands, of his work in the resistance, of his young wife, his one child, and home. He spoke of the goddess and of her old mother, her guard. Four or five islands stood always within the horizon, and Kimon named them, pointing; once, near Delos, he flew across a private beach, and the naked women waved.

The sea, from the angle of sun in the air, looked to Sotiris like paper, white with the small islands black. The sea straight below them, however, seemed transparent, shallow, blue, showing the lava formations and fish, showing the patterns of sand. Whenever they sighted a great school of fish, Kimon would radio in to the fleet, giving their type, their numbers, if he could tell, and place. Sotiris, grown used to the plane's glide and hover, stared at their white winking backs.

Why did I come here, and what will I do? How long have I lain here; how long must I stay—filling my belly with air? And where have you been all the night?

Sotiris, lying on his little bed, alone, looked through the window and out at the sky.

They could print a poster to say I was lost. Lost: One Sotiris Procopirios. Brown-eyed, black-haired, of medium build. Age, twenty years. Distinguishing marks: a brown spot on forehead (which I have not got, which they saw in a picture), black spot on right arm. Perhaps they have listed me missing from Rhodes—and all village boys with brown spots on their foreheads, with spots on their arms, will be assembled and shot. For running away. Deserting.

The sun was hot, already at seven, and his skin, wet. He had been gone for a week.

If Orsetta were dead now, they would want me back, the heir apparent who doesn't appear. To show them the money and lead them the way—perhaps on my poster there's: "Treat with Respect." Well, then, all village boys with spots on their foreheads and spots on their arms will be resurrected upon the third day. And he, my kind father (think of his face and glad look), will welcome me back and forgive. I had failed in the long line of duty; he asked me recovered, he printed up posters—but all is forgiven again. A party, perhaps, when I come. A party with singing and flowers and everyone there, turning the lambs on a spit, expecting to be very rich.

Sotiris saw his island covered high with slag, growths upon the sterile earth, great gaping holes each hundred feet where someone once had worked, brown grass beginning on the hills where nothing more could grow. Spades like violated crosses marked the bottom of each mound.

Starved sheep and pigs with folds for ribs snuffled searching near the pits, fell, and could not rise; horses rooted
fruitless fields for husks and chaff, all grain long gathered,
lost. Men, weak and fainting, came to sift the rubble for
its gold and fight for turnip rinds. Famine surprised the
land. The last litre of oil was poured, the last preserves
unwrapped. Dried figs became the only food and finally
were gone. The slag heaps shifted monthly, came at last
to rest. Men fell upon their animals and, eating, died
diseased. Swollen, pitted, pock-marked, bare, the digged-
up island seemed a single dug.

The next things that he came to know were hunger and
mistrust.

Phillipos Stritsas was thirty-two years old, and those who
met him thought him twenty-five. "I am forty," he said,
and showed a missing tooth. "I am in my old age." And
those who met him laughed. His eyes, as Sotiris', were
brown and long hair black, his nose was straight, ears
small. His family was rich; he never kept a job, but went
home once a week, to have the servants clean his clothing,
or to collect a book. The book he then would keep. And
once a month, on Saturdays, he ate dinner at home, wearing evening clothes, the black tie tight around his neck,
sitting between his mother and old father, telling them
his plans. The plans were never real; he had to think of
them that afternoon, enter them in a chart—a plan to
start a magazine, or make a rocket fuel, or lead an expe-
dition to the Congo after masks.

His mother did not care; she loved her only son and

thought him a success—his father, senile and retired now, needed only to hear of plans, the details, problems, and hope of high profit; he never remembered to ask, the next month, at the next dinner: Well, and what results? "Variations on a scheme," Phillipos called the chart. For sometimes, dribbling, with white head bent across his shirt, Mr. Stritsas would scratch the table, say: "We have heard this before! Now what results, young man? Where is my faith in you?" And he would spill the food. Phillipos, therefore, was careful always to have different plans for the Saturday dinners, and write them in his chart; had he repeated one, his father might still know.

His father never knew, or no longer could prove, how much Phillipos took; his mother did not mind. "I wish you all success," she said, signing the check, "and come here soon again."

He lived alone, in the Placa, but had two bedrooms and a living room, a kitchen, remodelled toilet, and a dining room. He was a careful cook and often spent long afternoons preparing that night's meal, as special for himself as when cooking for friends. He cooked more expertly than all the women that he knew; hoping to make him dinner, they ended only by doing the cleaning, while he watched and drank. Before they came into his spare bedroom to see his Chinese knives, he always made them do the washing up. "Neither empty stomach nor full kitchen sink," he wrote above the bed. And sitting, alert, they smiled.

He had other things to show from his former travels, and from his mother's kindness, when he stayed at home.

A drum covered in snakeskin, African gods with nails in their bodies and hands, camel bladders as gourds, a paper-weight of an elephant's molar, ivory horns and a jade cutting blade, Dufy drawings, Matisse prints, rich hanging rugs from Mexico and Persia, bright Indian bowls; care-fully, he cluttered his apartment, and kept it very clean.

Thin, and strong, with sculptured head and dark, low-lidded eyes, his having lived in Egypt and the Costa del Sol, his heavy boots and love of catching fish, his wealth and his disdain ("This is my town," he said, "I know it upside down," and stood upon his head), Phillipos had many women turn to him, for all of whom he cooked, to all of whom he showed his Chinese knives.

"Today it's plastic surgery," he thought, "to make a Greek a Turk, or Greek out of a Turk, then send them over to Cyprus as spies, or, more simply, disguised, to col-our a moustache and hook a straight nose high, to let a husband spy upon his wife, to play the postman, too, the rich far uncle seeming poor, arrived, to see where his photograph hangs, theatrical costumes perhaps, a stick for every hag, or make an old man young again and make the young men old—that should appeal to father, that should strike him well. But be more specific," he thought. "Think of the one from Rhodes. He looks exactly like, can come forward as proof. Of how the system works. An operation done to make another me. Yes, plastic surgery," Phillipos told himself. "I'll add it to the chart. Pretend to have a friend," he thought, "who is a surgeon now."

"*Saturday,*" he wrote, and rubbed his pencil point. "*June twenty-eighth.*"

"Chrysanthi ought to come. Or possibly," he thought, "she doubles with my double now."

"*Stritsas' Shop for Faces,*" he wrote across the sheet.

The last two years, Chrysanthi had been his, had stood upon her head with him and danced his minuet. His minuet was slow; at each uplifting of the arm, his partner took a drink, Phillipos humming to the tune and eating apples whole. "*Surgery,*" he wrote. But he had known, two days before, outside the theatre, when Sotiris spoke, that she would be absent again.

"*Change Yourself,*" he wrote. "*Free Consultation Fee.*"

Dust danced across the sun; Phillipos told himself: "He'll be my first exhibit, yes, newly arrived from Rhodes. She will not come," he thought. "I'll call another, and cook lunch; I wonder who he is."

Les Bluebell Girls and Dance with Lucas, stationary, winked; Sotiris heard again the body's plummet, scream. The widow Fontes, he remembered, in Soroni, at his birth, had built a mausoleum, huge and grey, for her husband and son. The shadow man before him lay, abandoned, near-naked, bent. Overlooking the valley where her peasants lived, hating her, for all her show and wealth, by the marble mausoleum, she died in November. Ten people, merely, came to the service, and, at the funeral, her lawyer had appeared with one thousand drachmas for everyone there; how sad the peasants were, the absent countryside, and, spiteful, how she paid for faith. With long white underdrawers tied and toothpaste in its mouth, no shirt, red toothbrush tangled in its hair, with rib cage clear in lamplight and the left knee raised, gold cross upon the concave chest and hand unopened, taut, the dog still howling terror-struck and curtains furling shame, Sotiris turned to run. A pack of policemen gave chase. The dead widow Fontes smiled victoriously from her bus; he left Rhodes like a great gamebird. No man gave food to him. Behind, black stone minarets skewered the sky; lamplight stretched a white arm on sea.

DANIA SARANDITIS stood in front of the old woman's bed, trying not to stare. She had not been there before. Wasted, Orsetta's white face looked like the sheet at her chin; the room was dark, silent, with flies lying dead on the floor. Black-clothed, behind her, stood Anna-Maria.

"What do you want?" Orsetta repeated. "What is it you want from me?"

Dania pronounced her name.

"So—Saranditis. And what is that—what is Saranditis? Who are you?"

She started to explain, started to tell that she wanted to help, had ridden her bicycle till she was weak, had come to Charaki to help—but suddenly she thought that Sotiris might never have mentioned her name.

"Well, what is it, Saranditis? What is it you want?"

Dania wanted only to run, to get back on her bicycle and ride into the sea. They did not even know her name.

"I am sick, girl. Go away."

But she managed, finally: "I—I knew your grandson once."

Orsetta tasted spittle, said: "I have no grandson. Go away."

"I saw him just before he left. Just those days ago."

"So—so what is that? I saw him too." Orsetta closed her eyes, leaned back.

"He is unkind," Anna-Maria broke silence to say.

"Was, he was unkind, not is! I have no grandson now!"

She had survived the month. Tomorrow, the next month would start. It did not matter now.

"I came to help."

Would the girl not go; could she not have peace?

"Well." Orsetta heard a fly. "Do you know where he is?"

"No," the girl said. "No."

They said the same thing. All of them; everyone who came. Anna-Maria put her hand out, but Orsetta raised herself alone and cried: "Then, Saranditis, go away!"

Dania turned and left. Orsetta fell back on her bed.

"Remember, Orsetta, when I was but seven," Sotiris thought, "you walked across the room, trying to teach me to see, to 'see with your insides,' you said. And then you closed your eyes, stretched your arms out, walking blindly, telling me you would 'fulfill yourself with red.' I thought, Orsetta, you would fall, or walk into furniture, and wanted you to stop—but, taking no notice, the same slow procession, you turned."

And backwards, into time, he turned his face again.

A pit, smoking, deserted, surrounded by sand, lies outside of Charaki: it is there the villagers leave their waste
and food. Bits of broken glass, an old chair, bone, bushes
torn up, and tires, food, forage for the gulls: all is thrown
into the pit, and, once a day, is burned.

Dania, leaning on her bicycle, stood at the top of the pit.
Afraid the smoke was a fire, passing near, she had merely
come to look, but stood unsteady, staring down.

As a little girl, once, playing queens and challengers,
alone, she had lost her balance, tumbled off the courtyard
steps and fallen, twisting her left arm, onto a rubbish pile.
Broken bottles, stone, ash and old food, sticks—she lay
there, in the middle, remembering the gipsy woman with
glass in her thumb who said that it never came out. Then,
finally, holding the painted wooden sceptre in her good
right hand, crying, unable to stop, she had climbed back
up to the house, where Mehmet Effendi comforted her,
where the doctor came to promise it would heal.

Flies clustered like grapes to the ground, hovered near;
a dead fish lay, blistering, pecked black. Dania stayed out
of the line of the smoke, watching the flies, wondering how
many hours it would take to bicycle home.

"When I was little, I was small," Chrysanthi told the
floor, "I climbed upon a stool to kiss my mother's cheek.
Will you remember me?"

He would remember every time they met; the first times
back in Rhodes, when he was but sixteen, the night of the

theatre, and words he said to her outside, the next day
when they met again, that night, the start of their trip; he
would remember driving up the coast, the sea sounding
always upon the right, would remember stopping to dance
to music from the car radio, outside, above a beach, and
every song, it seemed, was sung for them; Voula, Kavouri,
Varkiza, Anavissos, Laurion, he drove the lonely road,
stopping twice to kiss and look at her, telling her how
much she had for so long meant to him; surprised, too,
with her own memories, her recalling him, his hand upon
her low red dress, her hand upon his neck; remember the
last open hotel, at midnight, where they stopped, by consent, telling the owner they were man and wife, the red
room where they stayed, overlooking the sea, the first
night, and this day, inside, upon the narrow bed, their
love.

Arching swallows whirled with forked tails flickering,
insects their only food, caught flying and brought back to
nests, mud lined with feathers, with straw, three eggs still
unhatched and one but begun, on a cliff, in tree hollows,
by roofs. The cliff swallow, bank swallow, martin con-
verged, found moths, followed water, broke free.

"The wind is high," Chrysanthi said. "Look what it does
to trees."
Outside, the high pines bent; he listened to the wind.
"A little orange tree. . . ."
"And all I have is yours," Sotiris said to sheets.
On their first day, before him she stood, at the wide

terraced window of their first hotel, her red dress opening in back, her head in morning sun.

"Down on the beach," she said, "bent nearly to the ground."

Uncovered, on their bed, he lay and looked at her, said: "I have wanted you for these four years again."

He had fought in his dream. And in his dream he won.

"Four years," Chrysanthi said. "It must be four years now. You've changed, you know." She smiled. "Oh, very, very much."

Red circles were the papered walls. The window creaked and closed.

"In Charaki, when I asked"—Sotiris closed his eyes— "they said that you had gone, and nobody knew where."

"Well, now you know," she said. "I live in Athens now."

The sea below was loud; he willed his dream away.

It had been of a horse, the last dream of his sleep, a man upon a horse, and every time Sotiris sliced, the man had cantered off.

Heraldic, in the sun, Chrysanthi came to him.

"You are so beautiful," she said, and kissed his open hand. "You shouldn't mind it if I call you beautiful. Because you are, you know. I watched you as you slept."

Until at last, awakening, the man had run away.

"I never have seen anyone so beautiful in sleep."

"How many," he thought, "have you seen?"

He watched his covered feet, their lines in the long bed.

"And I am truly yours," she said. "I truly was last night."

He wondered, would she lie?

The man had worn black boots, had ridden a white

horse. With black whip in his hand, he had reared to the
sky.

"And here I am," she said, "with all permission yours."
The window opened, hung.

Sixteen, at the festival, hopelessly in love with Chrysanthi,
longing and alone, Sotiris was drawn to the house where
he knew that the girls would make ready, dress themselves
in preparation for the dance—where she would be perhaps. And on some small excuse, intending to ask Efi
Christodopolous if her father had come, he opened the
door to walk in. There, holding her clothes by her side,
wearing nothing at all, stood Chrysanthi. Naked, she
looked at him and then ran away down the hall. He did
not dare to follow her, but stared at her buttocks and
shoulders and thighs; she had made no movement, not
even to cover her stomach or breasts, had simply turned
and run from him.

Later, at the dance, in the glow of fires and the smell
of roasted food, holding his knowledge close, he stood in
the shadow staring at her, she who was the center of all,
laughing and dancing with everyone there, accepting gifts,
head thrown back and silk heels caressing the grass—he
stood until she came to him, she, Chrysanthi, asking him
to dance with her. He stammered no, he would not, and
she asked him why, standing in front of him, tapping her
foot.

By some right of possession that he could not understand, she was truly his that night because he had seen
her; perhaps the others girls had teased her into claiming

him; perhaps she, too, had been aroused—but her holding him tightly out in the fields was no more than conclusion to his having seen her undressed. He had stumbled upon her; she made love to him—and the act was completed, bound; he could have her no more. Chrysanthi was to leave unanswered his constant, unasked questions: the naked look of her face on that night was clothed and covered again. He knew the sordidness of loss, the sudden crumbling of his hope not that night but the next, when he went to see her and she was not in.

Festival over, he walked, in the cold wind, to the fields, looking for bent grass where they had lain, but found no trace at all.

"Distinguishing marks," he said to the sky. "When I was little, I was small. . . ."

"A farmer had three daughters, but loved the youngest best, for she was lovely, gentle," Sotiris said, his hand upon Chrysanthi's arm, "and kind. Returning from a market journey, bringing presents home, he stopped to pick a rose, for that was her present, for only that she asked, the others having asked for lace and rings. It was a private garden, where the roses grew, and suddenly a monster took his hand.

"This is a tale," Sotiris said, "my grandmother would tell, when I was six or so, at night, to make me sleep."

Chrysanthi smiled at him, uncrossing legs again. Crumbled biscuits, honey, streaked her plate.

" 'You are my prisoner,' the monster said, 'and I will eat you up.' The farmer begged and begged: 'I shall return,

I promise, and then you can eat. But let me take this rose home to my youngest daughter, that she remember me. Let me take ring and lace.' The grey monster agreed, claws huge in his furred hand. They swore a solemn oath."

Chrysanthi raised her arms. He heard her last night's cry.

"At home, the farmer handed presents out, then said that he must leave. The elder two sisters were glad, wearing their rings and lace, and asked him each for bracelets on return—the youngest shed hot tears. 'You are never with us,' she said, 'and seem so troubled now.'

"He took her in his arms to say farewell, apart, and told her how the rose had been enchanted, how his death must come. He had promised, he said, and would not break the oath. Not even to a monster, grey and furred."

"Not even to a monster, grey and furred." Chrysanthi grimaced, clawed.

" 'I shall come, too,' she said, and would not change her mind. 'It is for me you die.' "

Closing his eyes, Sotiris saw Orsetta's face of disbelief and scorn when, years before, telling him the story, she spoke about the oath. Terns screamed above them, and she said, "Remember, never swear."

To her, however, he had sworn, a week before, in Rhodes.

"They journeyed to the monster's garden, each silent, each in grief. Arrived, the daughter cried: 'I sacrifice myself for you,' and said to the monster, 'Kill me! It was for me he stole your rose; I wear it in my ear.' "

"And the monster agreed"—Chrysanthi laughed—"because she tastes better. Being a beautiful girl."

"The monster turned into a prince, and kissed her on
the ear, where still she wore his rose, saying, 'The magic
spell is broken! Will you marry me? Such faith and faith-
fulness I never yet have seen.' Behind the garden, a great
walled castle appeared; six carriages came for them, drawn
by unicorns, and the two elder sisters each became a bush.
They all lived happily."

"Come, sleep, and carry him to wherever you will—
bring him to your vineyards, and to your gardens," Orsetta
sometimes sang. He kissed Chrysanthi twice. His open eyes
saw hers.

Apelis notified police that Sotiris was gone, had him
declared a missing person, his description sent. A picture
of Sotiris circulated the Sporades, in Athens, and on Crete.
A policeman in Athens, therefore, having seen the picture,
stopped Phillipos on the street, then radioed to ask when
Procopirios had in fact escaped. Phillipos overheard, was
able to prove himself a resident for years, identified himself as Stritsas, left. The policeman said, you correspond
exactly, fit another man described. Phillipos was impressed.

That afternoon, together, on the beach, Sotiris and
Chrysanthi walked among plastic and rock, the litter of a
boat. And, as they sat upon a rock, a dolphin wallowed in
to die. First, he thought it was a shark, and then he saw
the tail and fins, saw the bottle nose. Mottled, fat, eight
grey feet, drifting slowly with the tide and coming in to
land to die, the fish bled from the tail. Too weak to strug-
gle with the waves, it had followed shoreward a small shoal

of fish and cut itself upon the rocks, unable to return. Now, old, it flapped upon its side, the lines of its face a perpetual smile, caught in the shallows and reddening waves, skin losing colour because of the sun, too heavy to drift back to sea.

Sotiris, with no hope of reviving the fish but no other way to be kind, kicked water over its body and great creased smile; then, helpless and watching for sharks, they sat on a near rock to wait. The dolphin was a long time dying, with short liquid noises, agonized tail, and always-opened eye: sometimes it would lie quite still, gathering strength, then, bloody and thrashing, go desperate again.

Gulls circled on the sea, and Sotiris, to keep them away, threw small stones up in air. Two hours they sat there, unable to move, not knowing exactly when the fish died, but recognizing death. The sun began to set, and, because of clouds, seemed a wing on wind. When finally they left, and circled back along the beach, it was to his first questionings, to their first night of loss. The drink at dinner tasted of dead meat; Chrysanthi said: "I've changed." He answered: "I, too, change."

She turned toward him then and cried: "You don't know, don't, and cannot understand!" Not once, in their three months, would he hear that again. Not once, in their three months, would he have heard as much.

A snuffle, whine, and sudden scream, repeated, a whistle, a moan, a dog barked, broken, terrorized, and faltering up to its high howl again, demented, hurt, invisible, somewhere within the square. Leashed white hackles strung to lamplight quivered by the Turkish Baths; a poster floated down. Wheelbarrows filled with rubble chorused to the cry. Sotiris covered with his heart her hand and scarved the waiting neck. He watched a yellow moth. As howling continued, insistent, the man looked out again, saw Sotiris, fell. Phillipos asked: "Why are you wanted? What is it you've done? A policeman stopped me yesterday to ask." Sotiris turned away, feeling not guilt but shame. He did not cross to where the man had lain, abandoned, half-naked, dead; he ran down the hill to the sea. Moths copulated on the wharf. Blessed splinters pierced his ear five times. Phillipos offered shelter, and he was forced to accept. The low floors of the buildings stood in darkness, while turrets of the buildings caught the light. Men playing távli beneath the stopped clocks looked at him, pointed, and cried.

BEWILDERED, twenty-three, Apelis had gone to Pittsburgh, and lived there seven years. When, by 1935, with the worst hunger passed, he held onto a job, it was as a house handyman, a servant to the rich. Apelis walked a basset hound, entangled in its leash and following the upraised tail two measured feet ahead. Apelis cleaned the car for them and took the child to school; he washed the kitchen doorstep down and painted all the stones. He watched the cook cook dinners, wore blue fitted clothes. He counted silverware, took the telephone, but then was ordered not to as his accent was too strong. "Sneaky Greek," they called him at the river bars. "No speaky Greek to me." And when Orsetta sent informing him she'd come, he had insisted no. She came, and his employers were away, gone for a quick trip West, and he pretended, therefore, that the house was his.

He took her arm when crossing streets to shield her from the cars; he brought her ice cream sandwiches and nuts. The busses frightened her, and trains; she dictated letters, awed, and he provided stamps. When finally she left, leaving him her little money and cursing her daughters-in-law, Orsetta was convinced that this one son redeemed all the rest. He looked at the Monongahela, saw his island home, and in the great smokestacks envisioned grey caïques. Later, he was to wonder if she ever guessed, if the treasure, meant for him, was her mark of mistaken respect, or but an old kindness delayed. She knew, he told himself, his mother surely knew.

Upon arrival home, Apelis had intended to tell truth. But when he came, a conqueror, with all the village standing at the dock, with flowers and Malona's band, to see him safely down, he could not kneel before Orsetta, or his father; his letters had preceded him, bore witness to success. At the welcome dinner and the welcome dance, his frightened silence made for faith; when he grew finally boastful, it was to unquestioned belief.

Knowing English, he easily obtained good English cloth; all tourists bought from him. His garment stores, respected, grew; he married, a success. But Nicoletta, prostrate, he never learned to raise.

HOME FOR SOTIRIS in Athens was by the Oros Koymapianoy, beneath the Lofos Strefi, leading up. In a tavérna once, he met a fisherman who told him of the room, costing thirty-eight drachmas a week, and he had taken it the next day without ever seeing the landlord, because there was no landlord living near ("He lives in splendour," said Theoni, "with ten cigars a day, and owns all of the street"), from Christoforos, cobbler, who possessed the key. Because his room was two flights up, the highest in the yellowing house, he could see the pines of Strefi hill, a bit of Lykavitos, and the constant sky. One flight beneath, down wooden stairs, outside Katina's room, there was a bathroom with running water, and also a pump by the rear chicken pen. Sometimes, at night, when tired, coming home, or having to set off for work, at dawn, Sotiris washed in the pump and listened to the chickens clucking, angry, or a cock, distended, loud.

The side streets coming down between the Lofos Strefi

and the Leoforos Alexandras are all made of dirt, deeply
rutted, steep, with garbage in the ruts and chickens pecking opened oranges, with shutters closed to sun. Dogs lie
upon the roof, in shade and under tires, by bottle crates
and clothes. The clothes dry quickly in sun, but then must
be beaten for dust, and women, neckerchiefed, lean out of
windows, beating their carpets and brooms, hitting walls,
holding breath against dust. Filth covers Yorgo slowly
as he sits in peace, not selling pistachios to the poor people
near, not trundling to the Leoforos Alexandras and the
busy streets, but squatting by his barrow, beating time.
Only a few cars pass, and very few attempt Koymapianoy
Street, which grows narrow and blasted and steep. Sometimes a man will come to hawk small fish or squid, singing
endlessly that they are fresh and cheap; sometimes a man
will pass out postcards of himself, with hair down to his
shoulders and a shepherd's crook, calling that he is the
last of the Misolonghítes, but more often there is silence
or noises that come from inside, a rooster or a cat, con-
struction at the red-rimmed windows by the boulevard.

Somewhere above the park of Ares, strident, incomplete,
someone played on an accordion, the same song, earnestly,
at three o'clock that night. Returning from her house
("You have to go," Chrysanthi said, and spoke her good-
bye as farewell), he passed the Green Park and Whiskey
à Go-Go, deserted now, the dying song beginning once
again, catarrhal, diminished and sad (for she had called
to him as he stood in the hall, saying turn around; he did,
and then she summoned him, one finger caressing the bell,
a white silhouette with her foot and her hip, one eye

sufficient, one behind the door, but tired he had left), and wandered the elegant paths by perfect statuettes. Past green-painted benches, the circled-in-grotto, flower beds and bushes he walked, the pavement watered down and small mimosa trees, the boarded stalls in silence, out into the street. A peacock once displayed itself, flown from the Royal Park for only them, it seemed, disdaining peahen for Chrysanthi, and there, by the three-sided, white, high column of Athena standing guard, gold-helmetted and stiff, her great cat underneath, he came into the Avenue, the Leoforos Alexandras, still busy at three in the morning, and still the accordion choked to begin, with HOOVER on his right and ALFA-LAVAL opposite, he crossed to start the climb. Chrysanthi would come there but rarely; always it was his, the pilgrimage, the starting at her house and final discharge of the door, her street, Mavromateon, broad and quiet, he, the stranger there (by the Italian Embassy a man with a monocle wept, disjointed, old, and fumbling worry beads, but then, the next day, Sotiris had seen him alight, chauffeur-preceded and calm, to enter her high house), then cutting through the park in early morning peace, a pigeon sleeping and his echo all the other steps, till out again to noise, a Vespa and a truck, a water hydrant spitting and the hum of lights, a frightened, dreaming dog, and the accordion.

Mehmet Effendi sat in a café, a Turkish coffee balanced in his hand. Before him, on the table, stood a glass of water, empty now; a little ring of water wet the table top. Noiselessly he mourned because he could not get another;

one coffee, and a single water glass, no more. The coffee, he could feel, was growing cold. Soon he would have to drink it, then take time with telling fortunes from the grounds, but that, also, would pass. Because of Cyprus, as he was a Turk, the Greeks no longer bought him coffee, nor called him Effendi for fun, he was no longer luck—and, as the owner neared, Mehmet Effendi sighed. He was allowed one coffee, out of charity, a single water glass, no more. And Dania's dowry must not be disturbed, he thought, I must not use it up. A cup can overflow. The glass of water, beaded still, began to speak to him. Mehmet, depart, it said. He put his hand upon the droplets, silencing, then wiped his face with the wet hand. He plucked at his moustache. His Dania was at home.

Beyond them all an osprey soared, wings spread above a silver fish, claws hidden, sunk in flesh.

Upon the *Myrtidiotissa,* steward in the second-class bar, not having seaman's papers and told to be content, Sotiris worked till one at night, dispensing coffee, pills, and blankets, opening windows in heat, and it was always hot, with deck chairs for those passengers who slept the short night through, not having paid for berths, the black-clothed women stretching full-length on their seats, chewing garlic, sick, a towel on the mouth and little paper baskets by their feet, with wicker baskets covered and a suitcase on the floor, and, at each port, the vendors came, selling loukoúmia and nuts, or medals, charms, and drinks, white boxes wrapped in cellophane with rose-petal candy inside. At one o'clock he left, locking the door behind, leaving his steward's jacket on the coffee trays, and wandered to the deck, to men who bartered lottery tickets, men upon the floor and babies blanketed, the fishermen and families all heavy-eyed, awake, and sprawled across their bicycles in sheets, beside the engines if it rained and under awnings, loud, himself, Sotiris, on the high deck, by the darkened string of lights and thinking back to Rhodes, the stops at Mykonos, small boats over the side, and then harbour police, the windmills and the bright white houses, waterfront cafés, in Syros, Tinos, Samos, all the Cyclades, and every three days back again to Athens in the dawn, Piraeus blue and busy-seeming, taxis at the pier and porters vaulting monkeylike for speed, a cargo ship unloading under cranes, to finding her alone, to his unchanging room.

"With golden jewelry, with pieces in faïence and paste, small figurines of ivory and gold, a funerary mask, grave markers, grey and mirror-shaped, a tusk and diadem."

Phillipos' father stumbled and said: "Where?"

They stood before a fire, with the windows closed. Phillipos wore a dinner jacket, black bow tie.

"The National Museum," Mrs. Stritsas said. "And what about the statues, did you see the statues too?"

"Málista, yes, and every single vase. But let me finish with the female heads, the entrance rooms, at least, with pins and pottery. There is a Mother Goddess, mother, looking just like you, and terra-cotta dolls. Bronze daggers and bronze cups."

"What are you talking of?" his father, white-haired, asked. "Have I heard this before?"

Phillipos spread his hands. "So you don't want to hear?"

His mother fanned herself. "We always want to hear."

"Because," Phillipos said, "the statues all looked very much the same. And therefore I decided we should too."

"And you decided what?" His mother opened eyes.

"Masklike, serene," he said. "I have a surgeon friend."

"Just talking on and on." His father's white head, lifeless, hung.

"No, truly, come from Rhodes. And we will build a business, I promise you, for masks. Greek gods again, all young, and all of us the same."

At ten o'clock they ate, with candelabras lit.

Sotiris, in his room, reached for Chrysanthi's hand and fingered air again. The first two weeks were simple for them, lovers and alone, spent wholly in the city and at night. He had Orsetta's money yet, taken from her wall, and with it they would eat, or drink by the Acropolis, out in the open-air bar, with ouzo and Metaxá for a meal, the lights changing above them, recorded Persians setting fire to the Parthenon at nine o'clock each night ("Sunny lumière," Chrysanthi said, "call me Brigitte Bard-oh"), a red reflected glow, and cars driving into the Pnyx (where once, in the small chapel, garlanded and brown, a man and woman married with flowers in their hair, a ribbon round his head, as he and she looked on, outside the entrance window, listening to love). They climbed the high hill, Lykavitos, slowly, to see the dying light, to stop beyond the path with crumpled cactus growing and a sad dog tethered to a spine, to reach the top in wind, where candle droppings clung and scattered Easter egg shells in the rock, bright red against the grey, with marble markers telling them the view, and telephone numbers etched in, and names. A little Arab woman in the chapel prayed to return, to good St. George, she said, her sacrifice each year was to ascend the steps, where once Athena, seeing eagles, dropped the heavy hill, not reaching the Acropolis because of augury, but dropping her earth load as eagles had appeared, the city spread before them, streets outlined to the sea, her house and his near-seeming and the Lofos Strefi dark, then down again in darkness to the low white lights, the steep steps where he held her and she left a shoe. A woman ordered chickens to sleep and children sold iced drinks, or in Tourko Limano, sitting by the sea, with a one-legged man and guitar ("You'll play for me," she said, and he had promised yes, had borrowed the guitar and sung her island songs, the beggar banging crutch and cup and humming his delight), two bottles together they drank and weaved among the boats where men dropped lines for bait and sold barboúnia, the bus ride back again, and on her balcony, reminding him of Rhodes, she wrapped her arms and legs around him, laughed and laughed.

Then roseate and vague, the future stretched before him: far away as sunset, changeable as sun.

CHRYSANTHI, seeing them both so alike, would often warn herself to not confuse the two. She held them separate. "They fight for each other with me— they fight with each other for me." She schooled herself to silence, anticipated mistake. "To err in humans is inhuman," Phillipos pronounced, then stuck out his tongue, asked: "My name?" She knew him by his speech. She felt them watching her; she spoke with the same voice to each; she noticed clothes and catalogued gesture; the same man took her twice.

Fifteen, Sotiris had seen Athens once before, had visited Andreas in the Polytechnion; it had been winter then, and Athens lay in snow. Visitor for one day only, taken across by Manos on a short business trip, he walked the city streets, aimless and lost, alone, then waited by the great square buildings of the Polytechnion, brick beneath the snow, for his brother to come.

Andreas was married with much ceremony and by the

bishop of Rhodes. Aliki wore white with a long flowing train; Sotiris, the best man, held candles as she came, the candles wrapped in lace. He held the blessed crowns of orange-blossom wreaths; he placed them on his brother's head and on his brother's bride, exchanging them three times and letting the ribbon fall free. He felt his collar slip. He watched them walk three times around the table, gather candied walnuts, kiss the Bible and the bishop's hand, drink wine together and bow for a blessing, watched the ushers stand and bridesmaids shift weight in their line; wearing stefanotis, he watched his brother wed.

Andreas rushed to welcome him, at the college, by the fountain where icicles hung from the little boy's lip; he spent that night upon Andreas' couch, shivering and proud. His brother's friends had gathered for a drink, coming to meet him, in the little room, showing they knew of him, that Andreas would often speak of how well he could swim, and sing, how he played the guitar.

Later, at the party, dancing with each of the bridesmaids in turn, he saw his brother fingering Aliki's veil and holding her ringed hand. In the ritual dance they performed, Andreas' forward steps had stayed within a circle, circumscribed, and in his smiling face Sotiris saw payment deferred.

Andreas had studied to be an engineer, had been a good student, eager for the work. Standing in the snow, he had offered his coat up for warmth. After a year, however, Apelis had recalled him, said: "You work for me, here, in the shops." Aliki awaited a wedding in Rhodes. And, out of loyalty, Andreas renounced the Polytechnion and engineering, left Athens forever behind.

THE OCTOPUS BEFORE HIM wallowed in its oil, and all the bread was gone. Bamboo bent in upon them, and electric candles swung; he ate an olive, drank, and turned in pillowed chair (the while the festival, with its trumpets and drums, its little village band, unrolled within Sotiris' drink, its bugles missing tune, and his remembered hope) to watch the singer's back. She had a C of velvet stretched across her dress and holding it in place; the dress was yellow, bursting, and the letter black. Chrysanthi offered wine. A flashbulb blinded him, and someone said: "For you?"

"You beat an octopus," Sotiris said, "to make it tender, soft." She curled the bottle back and handed him his glass. He took it, toasted her, and saw the dance again, saw ribbons and saw drums, her heels upon the grass. "And now," Phillipos said, "I want to ask your help." A bad guitarist plucked two-fingered at a string, and the blue light went red, the singer raising arms, her fat moving face like a fish and buttocks bouncing syncopated beats (in a green velvet shirt, their waiter, mournful, slow), a violinist then began the second song. "You are the one," she sang, "who makes my evening day." Phillipos took his arm. "I need your help," he said, "about my family." Again the bugles drifted down misplaced upon the wind; again Chrysanthi sat soft-heeled upon the grass. "And never ever run," she sang, "a world from me away." "A greenback dollar," Sotiris could hear, "that's what she offered me, and asked for a discount." Phillipos had suggested that they meet.

Red-haired she was, the singer, yellow-backed, with polka-dotted shoes. "To have you holding me," she sang, "is how I have to be." And arms like octopi, four couples took the floor. He watched a candle flicker, die, and saw his Dania dance "O mio bel amore" ringed with little girls, by black shell phonograph and badly whitewashed walls, the record, endless, rotating, until it wore away, until it scratched to silence, and the needle, blunt, left every song unsung. "My father," said Phillipos, "wants a proof this time." "If ever I should leave you"— ("Funny," thought Sotiris, "my father once did, too")—"I never would deceive you," and yellow light went green. Upon his back, by butterflies, Sotiris watched the sky. "So then it's settled," said Phillipos. "Thank you very much." A piece of feta crumbled, and he rolled in gorse, in thistles and in weed. "What's settled, then?" he asked, and bled above the knee. It was a wordless humming now, and polka-dotted pats; she reached the low note, faded, broke, and lifted arms again. "That you will come tomorrow,

to my house, to help." "To help with what?" he asked, and
saw Chrysanthi smile. "Don't smile at me," he said. "To
help with what?" But they had left to dance, Chrysanthi
in Phillipos' arms. Ice water fell beside him, and a waiter
cursed; immaculate, in velvet, another brought the pitcher
back and bowed away, mistaken, bearing fruit. Inside
Chrysanthi's glass, he saw her shape of lips and red-
rimmed, on his back, saw butterflies again. "Why will you
always hurt yourself?" Anna-Maria asked, and tied the
bandage tight. "Answer me that for once." "You are the
rose of summer and the rose of spring; your petal is of
metal; you bring everything." At the forgotten line, the
lyrical mistake, her violinist stared and pizzicato stopped.
"It was an Eastern wind, imagine that," Sotiris heard.
"Of course the ancient tiles were useless by that time."
And far away, above him, Chrysanthi, pinioned, rose.

"Remember the woman I met in the street, awaiting a
ride to come back into Athens—she, too, had a brown
beauty mark. Remember the way it came off her at night
when she sweated beneath me it streamed down her face.
And how in the morning she painted it on. Maria. My
Maria of the painted beauty mark, the 'treat with respect
although you find me in the street,' the 'wash yourself
well in my house,' of the house in Glyfada with two little
children, both of them used to their mother with men and
bringing us breakfast while we were in bed, knocking
first. Maria—I wish I remembered the way to your house."

The rain-slicked tiles were slipping, unstuck, underneath his feet; a row of anchor rocks dropped clattering
away. He clawed at edges, record smooth ("O mio bel

amore," with no lasting handhold at all), and fell the ten feet down, his ears in cherries still, and cherry branches breaking with his fall. Orsetta screamed and ran to him; he floated up again, toward the white treetops, the pillow of her arm, and from his childhood height he wished upon her peace.

"Your elbow," said Chrysanthi, "is covering my spoon." He offered them more wine and plucked the feta free. "The point of it," Phillipos was saying, "is in fact your skill. Just say you were transformed to look like me, find it pleasant, know the surgeon well. He won't ask more than that, I promise, and will soon enough forget." Her back was bending, wet, to curtsy seven times. He counted them and clapped.

Above him, on the second floor, they called for further sand. "Yes, yes," he answered, "yes." He took his shovel, lifted, threw, and falling stepped aside. He hunted octopus. He swung it at a stone. White dust cascaded down to pillar him in sand; he bent again to dig, hearing the call for more, this hopeless hauling earth, for him to try again, from up where they would build. Beneath his shirt a pebble stuck and scraped his covered back; he raised another shovelful and flung, then saw the dog-shark eye, and saw the dolphin smile. Chrysanthi took his arm. "I cannot say," Phillipos said, "how kind of you this is." He drank and stood again in Karaponou Street, Glyfada, by the yellow church with its twin safety lights. Within the bus stop he had waited, sheltering and wet, the first week of his stay, and there Maria found him, offered him her house. The shutters opened to a eucalyptus tree from which hung children's swings, and still the rain beat down, and the loud army planes landed behind her bed; her husband died in Canada, she said, and since then, holding him, announced she'd never been the same, her beauty mark dissolving down her cheek, and, unlocking the door, she told him to clean hands.

"I think we've had enough," Phillipos said, "bloodied brother," and the three of them were clambering up steps, past photographers and hats, into the empty air. "Who goes with whom?" Sotiris asked, and whinnied at a wall. "The three of us together, from now on."

The fifth thing that Sotiris learned was how to hire, sell.

Apelis and Andreas dug together ten steps from a fallen fence and twelve steps from a tree. The earth was hard and crusted, clear of stones and roots. "A swineherd sat here every day for years," Andreas grumbled, flailing with his pick. "How deeply could she dig?" He cracked the claylike soil, then crumbled it with spades; he rested while Apelis lifted the load free. They worked for two hours, where Orsetta said, when she had summoned them, and did not find a thing.

THE THREE OF THEM, together, spent one month. Sotiris, the next Saturday, and pliant for Chrysanthi's sake, subservient, went to the Stritsas' house, at Phillipos' request, and in Phillipos' clothes. "The Stritsas Shop for Faces," Phillipos had proposed, and, laughing, made him echo it for wine. But the old man was sick, and Mrs. Stritsas asked them nothing, said how much they looked alike, and nothing more was said. Sotiris left at ten. The next month, Phillipos spoke of figs, exporting fruit to Switzerland on ice. And his mother agreed.

"For services rendered," Phillipos announced, the next time that they met, and brought Sotiris wine. Chrysanthi watched him pay. He paid for everything, the Arizona club, the drinks at Zonar's nightly, and the Placa meals. He paid for gasoline, and it had been his car, the Lancia that they drove for their first days alone.

They still had days alone, when he would leave them suddenly, or not join them at night ("Munificent and kindly," read Phillipos' note, "I leave you to each other and escape"), but far more often, then, it was in crowds they met. In full supervision, patrolled, Sotiris walked with her near to the Zappeion, to meet Phillipos' friends, stake-centered, on a string: Kostas with his look of pure lust, Kostandis, the son of a furrier, with sable scarf and belt of astrakhan, a black cat catching goldfish in a pool, and Andonis beside ("The rich girls here," he said, and wheeled across the floor, "will slip away, here, to this room, and live as prostitutes. Sometimes they wear a mask"—he sighed—"and take whoever comes. Not me, I know this town," he said, "the crippled blacksmith me," and lifted hanging feet). Sotiris walked with her down dry grey marble halls, up stairs, skylit, to join another group, to lose her once again, seeing through open doors whole families asleep or in an argument, the men eating fruits and meat, reading the newspapers and lying back in beds, wearing their undershirts, or women at their work; would pass an old man walking sockless down the hall, to give and get no greeting, in front of him her legs; high-ceilinged and fine-floored, the marble toilets and baths of houses he entered behind her, the streets he could not place and names he never knew, not even to forget, the background voices raising into song ("And with the honey bees, Hymettos I have climbed," somebody saying, "climbed it barren-sloped," to play the lonely piano poorly as they hurried love), to leave the parties later, tired, drawn apart, no longer listening. ("And in the bus a man had drawn me, sitting opposite," Chrysanthi said. "I kept sunglasses on, not because he might think me famous, but

just in case he would not like my eyes and stop the picture. It was very flattering.") The piano whimpered
thumb-struck to a stop. He left her buttoning. A great
bloated body in pants, blue head beneath a photograph of
ships, picked up a narghile and told Sotiris: "Go. Do not
stay in my house." Obedient, he turned to weave the
passageway, to wander in the park, the people passing
birds, he thought, decided, storks, with flapping legs and
crooked craning necks, and, asking a deaf man directions,
following a leaf, he found the street, returned. Or, sanely,
on a Thursday afternoon, they walked together through
the Agora, or up on the Acropolis, it costing nothing then,
or Sunday, out at Daphni, with the poppies withering
upon their too-tall stalks, the three of them, together, on
a boat, and then Sotiris asking Phillipos if he had heard
of work, the next day, Phillipos arriving, promising it's
done (the little man with pince-nez and a pipe, behind a
metal desk who handed him, obsequious, a form and said:
"For Stritsas, yes. Endáxi!"), the *Myrtidiotissa* needed
stewards for the second class, and Sotiris could go.

He went (in a side room, quick physical he had to take,
a doctor reading off diseases and Sotiris shaking no, then
stuck for blood and stripped for broken bones, jumping,
naked, to show he could jump, bending, naked, to prove
he could bend), and, on the voyage out, three hours from
Piraeus, standing by a rail, he saw Chrysanthi in Phillipos'
arms. Phillipos, expectant-seeming, turned to see him and
then hurried forward to say: "There you are, finally, I
thought we'd go to Mykonos, and patronize the line. Favor
for favor, this world. What an elegant jacket you wear!"

Chrysanthi, by the lifeboat, watched him, in the wind, and Sotiris with buttons of brass held to his swinging tray. "Come cross the border, enter the first class, I'll vouch for you, no harm."

With the fog whistle blowing, tasting oil, he turned away to work, telling Phillipos no, telling Chrysanthi nothing, to distribute coffee and nuts, and later, Mykonos, when he handed her onto the ladder and the landing boats. Chrysanthi whispered to him quickly: "Please believe me, understand, I did not know that you'd be on this boat," and stepped beneath him down, her heels tattooing gone.

"**Y**OU CANNOT TELL ME what to wear," Aliki almost cried. "I know as well as you."

Andreas answered nothing, shook his head.

"I am fat already, see?" She pointed to her stomach. "Three months gone. I want a mother's dress tomorrow, and you should know why."

"Why?" Andreas said.

"Koúklamou, my doll, you cannot even guess?" Her voice changed to a teasing voice.

"No, I do not know."

"Oh come, kouklákimou, and guess." Aliki smiled at him, lifting her eyes and dropping her head. He wondered how to buy a dress, if there would be time. He wondered where his father was, and why the store was closed.

"You will tell me anyhow."

"Yes, yes," Aliki said, "but guess."

"Because you don't like the dresses that you have."

"Because," she told him carefully, "it will look well

for me to be a mother, to show Orsetta that I am with child."

"She knows already," said Andreas, looking at the floor.

"But to remind her, understand, in case she should forget. In case, in case," Aliki said.

No longer with the ship, no longer with Orsetta's notes, and needing money now, Sotiris looked for, found himself part-time summer work. Ten nights he worked in a restaurant near the Acropolis, cutting up salad and lamb, serving beer, vissináda, and wine, cleaning off tables and sweeping the floor. For this, he received dinners, a few tips, and enough money to pay for his room. Once, because of an argument, Chrysanthi came, as an insult, sitting with two men and one other girl, refusing to recognize him.

But he liked the dinners, liked sitting at eleven o'clock, under the looming Acropolis hill, eating the remnants of customer food and finishing half-empty bottles of wine.

For one week, later, he worked in an elegant beach outside of Athens, half an hour up the coast. Arriving at eight in the morning, his job was to clean out the sand: seaweed, bottles, suntan tubes, newspaper, small stones—he raked them to the border of the beach and left them there in piles; he unlocked cabanas and opened out chairs, posted the time of high tide. Then, lord of all he saw, Sotiris could swim, and, in the deep warm water, check the moorings of the raft, prepare the pedal boats.

But, as with the other job, after a time and some money

saved, he saw no reason to keep at his work—missed one day, another, and did not return.

"I do not wish to stay in bed," Orsetta thought. "No longer, now. I wish to see my man."

The walls were quiet, silenced by this time.

"My husband, my young man."

She had survived three months. Tomorrow, they would kill the calf. She wanted him to know.

"Come a little closer," she said to the air. "I am tired, truthfully, and cannot shout."

Apelis walked into the room. She could not see his face.

"Yásou, mitéra," he said.

She knew him by his walk.

"Anna-Maria, ya," he said. "How goes it here?"

"Not bad," she heard her sister say. "Not bad."

She had survived three months. Her husband ought to know. He sat there, huddled, in his coat, staring at the flames.

"Mitéra," Apelis said, "do you want something—anything—is there something I can do?"

She wanted the door closed again; why had he opened it?

Anna-Maria closed the door.

Fourteen rooms. A kitchen, pantry, dining room, the study where her husband sat, a living room and hall, seven bedrooms and a parlor, kitchen, pantry, dining room—a terraced walk out to the land.

"Something that I can do?"

The servants bringing food and drink, obeying her command. The shiftless peasant girls; she knew.

"Before tomorrow comes?"

He came toward her, bending down, his breath upon her face.

The richest woman of the town; Malona, even Rhodes. A fly was on the bed.

"Would you enjoy it if I quieted the walls?" The servant, offering.

"Nai," Orsetta answered. "Yes."

"Yes, what, mitéramou?"

"Mitéramou," she said. "Mitéramou."

He put his hand upon the bed; she felt the sheet grow tight. His picture hung above him, on the wall. She closed her eyes again, saw rooms.

Anna-Maria said: "Perhaps, Apelis, you would like a seat."

"Send father to me, boy."

Orsetta heard the calf.

"Your father to me, boy."

And then the days turned bad, a sudden rainstorm tamping dust and making women run, the doorways filled with waiting and the bread stalls soaked, beneath a MOTOROLA sign a taxi on its side, or in Athena Street, alone, the hopeless hawkers pushing him, and the meat-market streets, booth after booth of offal, kidneys, chicken, sheep, no sky above the awnings and red sawdust on his feet ("Your shoes," Chrysanthi said. "You have to buy some shoes"), their butcher aprons fat with flesh, with cleaving and with blood ("Just look at them," she said. "No leather left at all"), and liver on his arm, he stumbled to the chapel by the ochre church, and inside there were flies, beneath the chandelier, and out again were flies, a Bedouin in burnoose, with men selling candles and hats, a tractor shop and shop for plastic—*Scuba Diving,* said the sign, *Beneath the Waters, What?*—a little girl bent double in her room on newspaper, the Rivoli and Orpheus not open till the night, and in the gratings photographs of sheep, he saw a priest with sunglasses who limped and giggled past, a can of mastika, Ursus among the Wolves, the posters read, Les Bluebell Girls, and Dance, saw men shaking hands, selling dolls ("Buy me," Chrysanthi said, "to hang around your neck"), the desolating wind, straw chairs upon the pavement, embassies and flags, and finally a poodle wearing fur.

A caïque came to shore and dragged upon the beach. Apelis turned to go; she halted him again.

"And then this ring I give you, take it solemn mine," Orsetta said, "to change his wasting mind, to make it be as if his coming home, to truthfully at last be saying that is not the place, why lie, no, not the place, why worry longer when I come to measure money all was mine, to give him only this, a truth, and also there I failed. Because he would not stay."

Apelis took the ring and kissed her open hand.

From the Piraeus train that took him slowly back he

saw Phillipos' house, high on the Placa hill, a single yellow
light, and saw her sleeping there, in his mind's eye, content, beneath the Chinese knives and by Phillipos' side.
The empty, nighttime streets were heavy still with rain; he
smelled within himself an island seaweed smell. Chrysanthi had not come. Before the boat for Rhodes he waited
("Meet me there"—the fountain dying now he watched—
"we'll go together, if you do"), and she had never come.
"Forsake the high crest of your circlelike city; go live in
walls of wood," the oracle had said, during the Sound and
Light, the night before, as they watched, and she had
whispered yes, the promise but a lie. The Boulevard Tos-
sitsa, wide and flower-filled, became the Lofos Strefi, and
he was alone. BENAKI 105, a painted pointer showing
where the houses stood, beneath the little hill, creaked
cuckoo to the wind, and he would never tell how, trusting,
he had gone ("Come live in walls of wood"—her mouth
beside his ear) to wait for her in vain.

A row of pipes, enormous, mouthed at him through
fence, and then the dips of earth he wandered, in a quarter
moon, where men would shoot at birds, a filthy pigeon
pecking and the longhaired cats, low cactus, stunted pines,
wet grass beneath his feet (at ten o'clock, hospitable, a
watchman bought him beer, and it began to rain, and on
an oil drum, in a shed, he waited until one), and in the
nighttime now, policemen following ("Your circlelike
city is mine") who stopped to order halt (with the last
taxis leaving, porters changing coats, the boat behind him
lost), for when he walked away, they struck to make him

stop, to leave him lying down, their fingers back in belts, and the sweet-smelling rot of a grapefruit he faced, rain water in a rind, arose and found again his house beside the hill, thick blood beneath the pump, to hear her saying yes.

THROUGHOUT EXTREME UNCTION, Orsetta lay still, and after did not move. To help her die in peace, to ease her distant soul, Anna-Maria threw Sotiris' old shirt on the bed and called his spirit near to quicken the death agony, but, at the sudden added weight, Orsetta opened eyes. The shirt was red and torn. She understood and sat upright to throw it far away.

The meltémi, the north wind that blows all through the night of summer, swept the courtyards of the Old Town of Rhodes. Wind rattled at the shutters of the daytime shops, and wrapping paper battered at the sharp sides of buildings. Dania, in her room, bent to imagined work. She rearranged the pillows on her chair; she swept and cleaned the floor. She waited for Mehmet to come, for night. When he arrived, she would undo his coat, take off his fez, and ask him, carefully, if coffee had gone well. He'd say if he had been insulted, if they had been kind, or properly respectful, and tell her then of coffee as it was in Spain. He'd tell her of Gibraltar, swimming there from Turkey on a bet, of climbing it with camels and a horn. When he had talked himself to peace, Dania would tie his napkin to him, speak of her father, his friend. Then Mehmet would brighten, and holding fork and knife in his left hand drum upon the table with his right, imitating music and Alexis' bow.

Sotiris had not written to her, told where and how he lived. To him, in silence, she apologized, asked only that he break silence in turn, explain, complete himself.

Mehmet would smoke, and she would wash the dishes slowly, diagramming soap.

"I fear to give myself to you, cannot. I am afraid that, offered, I am not enough. I look in a mirror and see merely me. You see Phillipos in my every other face. The shame: always behind me, myself, and always watching, you. I am on a train—you, on the platform. Behind you moves another train. I think that mine is leaving, cannot tell the other motion from my own, yet you are always there, in front of me, down on the platform, ahead. Always I tell you farewell, always sure it's finished, and yet you follow, unmoving, a red handkerchief in your hand.

"This ought to be good-bye. This cannot end well, and it ought to be ended. You wore your hair up yesterday, and said my shirt was torn. It's memory, you said, that makes it hard to go; three months together make it difficult. Untrue. I had hoped that your hair would be down. It's memory that makes it hard to stay. We two are not enough; I had such hopes we were. And when you go don't turn. With you the best part of this place is gone, the street-danced festival is full of policemen for me. Love is diminished, done."

"**I** WANT TO SEE MY CALF," Orsetta said, "at once. Send her with celebrating me, for now is no delay. An apple on returning, to the pain. Go shepherd in his field."

They sent for Stavros, high up in the hills, and ordered him to bring the calf down to Charaki, garlanded and clean.

"Tonight?" he asked. "In darkness? Tomorrow is enough."

"At once," they ordered him.

He placed a hempen halter round her neck and locked the sheep in the sheepfold; he left the dogs on watch. Old men met him with torches, walked in front of him; Valeria was frightened, stumbling, and he talked to her: "This is no trip at all," he said, "for you and me tonight." Across a stream he carried her, slung across his back, where one man slipped and, falling, flung his torch. "No reason in the least"—Stavros laughed—"for falling, if you see."

They walked the wooden boardwalk to Orsetta's house, with village dogs behind and the sea loud upon stone; a woman garlanded the calf with red and white flowers, strung crosswise from her ear; they reached Orsetta's door. Anna-Maria said: "Bring the calf inside, please, Orsetta wants to see." But this he could not do; she kicked at the strong smell, the wooden door and lights; he had to lead her off, back down the boardwalk, pulling, inland from the sea. He left her with a man who placed his torch in earth, and walked back to Orsetta's house to listen to her wish.

"Kill it," she said, "and you for only kill."

He stared at her; she did not look at him.

"This morning is the last, and never came inside. You standing at the door."

"I have not got a knife," he lied.

"Sotiris losing all. Speak softly to him here."

"Valeria," he thought, "my little calflet now."

"Nobody, none at all. Put olive pits upon my heart as that is where it hurts, put garlic skins and wine. I have a knife," Orsetta said. "Kill with the bayonet."

He watched her try to move. Her eyes blinked twice and shut.

"It should be in the morning," Stavros said. "I should have men to help."

"In case they came," she said, "I will have hidden it. Hold tightly to the ear."

He saw the bayonet; Anna-Maria coughed. It was past ten o'clock.

"It's rusted, worn," he said. "It will not cut."

"You using it," Orsetta said, "and I command to now."

Garlands of flowers floated on the sea. The peasants all were drowned; she stood upon the rock, skirts lifted in high hand and offered him a grape, an olive pit, and fly.

"And show me it is dead. Show me the blood," she said, "for ever shall be here."

Stavros picked up the bayonet and left.

The party was in Phillipos' house, in the high Placa. The rooms were full and people noisy; he heard them from afar. He passed the fountain, the small yellow church, passed parakeets, a wooden trellis with beach beds outside, and saw the sun set three successive times. He heard the noise of feet, of some bouzoúki song. He climbed the tilted stairs; the bottom floor was boarded up and no one lived inside; before the door, a couple danced, and he stepped softly past. Looking for Chrysanthi, now, he saw her, on the far side of the room, and sitting on the floor. A girl came up to him, said: "You are such a perfect host, but now I have to go." Chrysanthi sat in a circle of men and women, all laughing, all intent. He watched them play a party game of catch; they threw wet slices of karpoúzi at each other, quickly, hoping to catch someone unaware. For if, Sotiris saw, the thrower missed his throw, he had to take a drink, but also, if the receiver missed his catch, he had to take a drink, and, as they both wanted the bottle, not the melon, sometimes they missed on purpose, but would then have to forfeit a turn, with everyone laughing and holding their hands out for wine, a great open retsina jug. Sotiris moved closer; a bowl of black olives was offered to him, crinkled skins in vinegar and oil. Chrysanthi caught the karpoúzi and threw; he had not realized she had noticed him, was not prepared, and felt it splatter on his arm, drew back. Somebody laughed; he smiled and reached out for a drink. She said: "Hello, again."

"You missed it on purpose," somebody insisted. "Who are you anyway?"

He did not take the jug. He saw the blue tiled patio of the church beneath. He turned to see Chrysanthi, but she was not there.

The next things that Sotiris learned were sleep, a weariness, the shadow of an action lost, and lust.

Stavros stamped out the light. He led Valeria behind the house, up past the pit prepared for roasting, the pit he had helped dig, into the first tall trees. The moon was very bright; his calf was calm, alone with him again, putting her nose in his hand. He passed her halter round a tree and dropped the bayonet, pulled the knife from the strap in his jacket arm and wiped it on his pants. Valeria began to graze and took two steps, stopped short, the halter growing tight. She switched her tail for nighttime flies, found none. Having no club with which to hit, he broke a branch from a fig tree, but knew it was too light and looked instead for stones. He found a round stone bedded in the hill and scraped it up; then, balancing, approached Valeria. "I am not doing this," he said. "Imagine it's not me."

He twisted a fig from the branch and gave it to her,

peeled; she licked it from his hand; then, with the other, upraised hand, he hit her with the stone. His aim was faulty, low; she buckled but had not been stunned; he hit her three more times. The fig fell unchewed from her mouth; she showed her tongue and grunted, twice. He lifted her head back and stuck the knife point in her throat, then sliced it, twice and tearing, cleanly to the side. She bled, in spurts and in a stream while Stavros touched her nose. Above, the ruined face sunk inward from the stone and one brown eye was blasted, all in blood; he dropped her to the ground and dropped his knife also, then wet the bayonet for proof and left, telling himself: "I'll have to get a pail and rope and someone's skinning knife. I'll have to sleep nearby."

Stavros tripped on a root. "Carrion crows," he thought, "should eat her insides out."

"TRÉHO, TRÉHO, I run."

Yorgo, the idiot, muttered in sleep, hands holding each other and feet curled up high, with string along the floor. One end of the string touched his toe; one was among the pistachio nuts; if they were to move, he would know.

The moon was full, and the Acropolis, open. Sotiris paid and stepped inside the gate, weightless, his feet in water, dry. The Parthenon grew huge, and those who passed him on the path held cameras aloft, rode bicycles, were cranes; he shivered in the wind.

Christoforos, cobbler, a basin by his bed, snored happily and held his leather whip. In his happy dream, the blankets were dresses, his room the maid's quarters, and he, the nobleman, inside. Sometimes the dream turned bad, and he became the maid, the master entering to find them there, together, in one bed, and whipping them till Christoforos screamed. But now, content, he slept and touched her with his foot.

Sotiris found a stone and fell, above the caves of Pan. Looking down at the street he saw in the cobblestones, snakelike, the urine of cripples unable to move all the day. A few sightseers stood, beneath the Pantheon or by the Sacred Way, but he was left alone, holding his stomach and head.

Thetis and Theoni, widow and sister, lay listening to silence from the room beside, Katina's room, on their sides to hear the better, breathing into sheets. A shutter creaked and curtains moved with wind; Theoni turned and said: "Aha, she's at it now." Thetis, toothless, agreed.

Below were the night-sharpened noises of Athens, a song from the Placa and cars. He heard the neon lights.

Katina was not home.

A long dog whistle blew, and his head bent in pain. Chrysanthi and the others were at play.

Outside Charaki, by the pit, a black cat turned to run. The bones of fish caught fire now, behind them flamed an olive tray, the far grass stood in smoke. A sea gull, startled, flew; as on every other night, lit by a villager, the pit would flame and sputter, burn its food to ash. Stavros, climbing the hill, passing the empty festival pit in which, tomorrow, he would cook, could see the orange sky and see the glowing distant flame, but all he heard was blood. He skinned Valeria with no light for the work. Orsetta had taken the bayonet, smiling, trying to wipe it on sheets; he had come quickly back. He finished cutting off her head and slung her from a tree, her forelegs hanging limp, then crossed himself, sat down. He covered the pail for her entrails

with a carob branch. He cleaned a hollow in the earth
and stretched beneath a bush, wind-covered, cold, com-
panionless. Driving his knife into the ground, he worried
for his sheep. If he had not been proud, had told of
Valeria's stomach disease the time the apple stuck, she
would not now be slaughtered, he thought, would never
have been used. He listened to the sea, telling himself he
could not hear the slow dripping of blood; he heard a
hooting owl.

A rope of goat's hair and a strap of goat's skin with a
hole; Sotiris held the sling, and, thirteen, flung stones at a
tree, or played catch with a friend, throwing in rhythm,
shepherd and a wolf. Accurate, he could hit high branches,
peaches sometimes, and another stone. Once, using a fig,
he hit Orsetta as she walked, then turned and ran for fear,
with her cry following, which he could hear again.

"For all the care you give," he said, and opened his
shut hand, "I could be lying here."

Now, looking up at the stars, the night sky, he sang with
the beauty of it; each crystal star that ringed the moon,
glimmering and changeless, overflowed for him. Upon the
incline of the slab, Sotiris lay suppliant, saw the sky his
cup. Great and overturned with drops of nectar clinging,
chalice of gods offered only to him—he took it, reverent,
drank deep, and willed himself in Rhodes and smiling
started down.

"A man sowed salt and hoped for a harvest. As luck
would have it, a hunter came by, and the man asked him:

'Why doesn't my salt come up after these months?' The hunter answered: 'Some beast must be eating it.' Just then, a grasshopper sat on the farmer's chest. He thought it was the beast, and, in his fright, he could not speak but pointed to his chest. There, the grasshopper sat; the hunter aimed and shot, hit both, and brought them down."

Andreas was asleep. Aliki, on the toilet, felt her rolls of fat. Looking up, half-risen from the seat, she saw her shapeless self reflected opposite; at dinner, he had laughed. She wondered, did he laugh at her, when, telling that story, he left. "He must have laughed at the story," she said. "Why else?" Now, staring at the mirror, one hand in the washbowl and one hand on her knee, with toy boats sailing down the wall and water on the floor, light webbing her lashes and splintering glass, tasting salt and lamb chop, rancid, in her throat, she cried about her marriage and baby-to-be, loudly, hoping Andreas would hear. He made no sound at all; she washed her hands again.

> *Down on the beach,*
> *down on the shore,*
> *down on the beach, kondí,*
> *a little, twisted,*
> *bitter orange tree.*

The marble hall resounded to Sotiris' walk. The long hall lay deserted now; one transom glowed already lit or still lit from the night. In forty minutes he had reached

Mavromateon Street and, the door not being shut, had entered her dark house. A milk bottle lay overturned and empty; arabesques of milk circled the floor, and Sotiris side-stepped. He went up to Chrysanthi's door, unlocked it, moved inside.

Sotiris looked at her, Chrysanthi, where she slept, and stood a minute, silent, telling her farewell. Her hands curled at her hair. He took a pencil from the desk and wrote upon a piece of paper: "Chrysanthi, I am gone."

He dropped his key upon the paper, placed them both beside the bed, and left.

Stavros worked, stiff with tiredness and cold, at lighting the great pit. The coals and wood lay wet with dew, under the sea wind. He sprinkled kerosene and fired the low branches of the pit, working in darkness, warmed himself with flame. The slow coals caught and smouldered, reddening the pit.

Oncoming cars were few; the city, derelict. Sotiris had sufficient money for a bus; a woman with a chicken was the only other passenger; he settled back to sleep.

The driver sang out stops they made, and, insistent, stopped at every second street, according to his schedule, with no necessity, as he was never hailed. The chicken, tied around its legs with a loose cord, escaped. Squawking, it flew across the bus, but hit its head against a window, dropped; the woman picked it up again and stumbled to her seat. Sotiris, at the airport, left.

THE PHONE CALL was finished. A spider had been dying in the booth; he watched it turn and fall. His father, awakened, would send money to the telegraph office in Athens airport, would meet him at the plane. He would be welcomed home. The celebration was to start at one; the calf would then be cooked, and all the guests arrived. Sotiris would be fetched as a surprise. Apelis did not question him, nor ask how much exactly the plane fare would cost, said simply: "Good, I shall meet you at three." At Sotiris' question about the police, Apelis seemed surprised, then laughed to explain: "Oh, yes, I sent them after you."

Sotiris took a drink. It was a water fountain for children, the only one he saw, and bending down to drink from it, he fell onto his knees. Kneeling, he sucked from the dribble of water, then slowly rose again.

A child, he used to place a stick upright in earth and spin himself around it fifteen times, then place the stick straight on a chalk mark in the wall: he always won the game; the other boys would fall, or, laughing, slip, or miss the mark by feet. Sotiris trained himself, alone, out on the beach, to whirl and turn so that the beach and sea swooped crazily to curve and sing with wind, to leap like waves to sky, so that the rocks beat down upon him and the clouds were sand, so that he danced like twisted string, a weight turning on rope, and, turning, still could stop, could walk away upright.

But now, walking away, he could not keep his balance, could not see the ground. It fell from under him, and rose, and hovered high; a cat biting its tail.

"With head beneath her feet and ikons in high nose," Orsetta was saying, "this love is troubled, too. No ship is lifted without waves," she said, and laughed at her small sister near, "and no least tree is rootless, toothless, mine. Why would a dog," she said, "cross streets to get to shade? Why should a bird have legs, to land once in my life? The shiftless peasant girls; I have a shift," she said. "Let me, when I die, smile; let you, Sotiris, come; you, the angel Gabriel, coming for the good. Take off your coat, I said, lie down before the door. And let me not see Michael, who collects the wicked; let me die on Sunday, please, for luck."

Sotiris walked out of the airport, down the airport drive, crossing the main road, stumbling through a tall, thick clump of grass. His head felt light, his stomach, heavy, and his ankles hurt; he fell forward and down. Awake, he lay with insects, the sweet grass sharp against his nose, the noise of cars a rising scream, and all his body shaking with the wait. A small tree gave him shadow; time passed, he lay in sun.

"Anna-Maria sleeps. You snore like seven wolves, and everything within the house hidden. My treasure will return, all clarified in old."

"It's Sunday, now," Sotiris thought, "for all the care you give. Chrysanthi going home." And he remembered then the early times of pain, of beating out hello, of "One, two, three, hello," to feel the word inside and opening out sound, the hum inside him held, of talking sentences to air, the hard, touched-only-by-him frightened lines at the sides of his mouth, and breathless, bowing: "Yes. Of course you can, pára polí ligo, a little, how are you, well, well, good morning, yes, kali andámosi, good-bye," a fat grey rabbit running through the trees and turning once to watch him, hopeless, raging, head between his hands, repetitive and still, and in the rabbit's mindless eyes he mirrored saw his own, of lying in his father's cave and singing out long lines, of practising, "My name is Procopirios," in tune, "I have a brother and no mother, take the telephone," of lying if the truthful answer would be hard to say, pretended sickness of the throat and all the little bargainings of fear, of breathing in and out, and water, pebbles, olive pits he took, of the thicket again and birds stuttering songs, of light between the leaves and saying, in the rhythm of two stones: "This is the way to win the world, this is the lasting love. I can go home to try."

And the remembered past, the little boy he'd been, turned inward on himself, was done.

Orsetta Procopirios, lying on her back, looked up at the ceiling, saw it, did not see it, and was dead.

PART THREE

rHODes

_____

"THERE IS A PEASANT LEGEND," Manos said, "a story I have heard."

He and Eleni were at breakfast; it was eight o'clock.

"The legend tells of village lovers, forbidden to wed. The girl's father forbade it—he was very proud—the others were too poor."

"Pass me the toast," Eleni said.

And Manos passed the toast.

"He was an unpleasant peasant," Manos joked.

He looked around the room. The room was small, with blue wallpaper, and a large window. The floor was of white tile; Manos looked at the floor.

" 'But I without him am a field without seed,' the rich girl said. 'Earth is the queen of beds.' 'Your boy must have some gold,' her father answered, 'golden seed. Now that is all. And bother me no more with talk. Say not another word.' "

"I wish that you would trouble me no more with talk," Eleni thought. "I wish I could have peace."

"A certain man," Manos continued, "had two fields. They rose above the village, on a hill. In one of them the lover worked; the other lay fallow. The fallow, level field would soon be used for corn."

Eleni took some jam. She spread it on the toast.

"Each afternoon at two, when he could rest from feeding pigs and picking weeds, the rich girl came to meet her love, to lie with him down in the fallow field. The father never knew this, and stood firm."

"It's an auspicious day," Eleni thought, "at least."

The furniture was white.

"One afternoon at two, the father wandered to the fields with his friend, the landowner. It was the day before they were to plant the corn. Coming upon his daughter in her lover's arms, he killed them both."

Eleni took another sandwich from the pile.

"You never listen to me!" Manos shouted. "What did I just say?"

"He killed them both."

"And just before that?"

"Daughter in her lover's arms."

"Well, do you think that happened; do you think that is the end?"

"The end of what?" Eleni said. "What will you wear today?"

Anna-Maria came awake with sun. It glittered off the ikons and a white enamel jug; outside, a sea of silver met the beach. Orsetta, in the high bed, lay upon her back. Anna-Maria stretched. She sat up in the bed. Out of the window, she could see the cloudless sky and a far fishing boat. The pebbles of the beach were white. She tried to count the stones in the stone wall that fronted on the walk. She could not, tried again. Again, the outlines blurred; she knew there should be seven, six nearest the gate, but could not tell their shapes.

"The glare is in my eyes," she thought. "That makes it hard to tell."

She lay back down again. Her left hand scratched her leg. "I saw the fishing boat," she thought, "and that is far away." She shifted her position in the bed. Her fingers curled up to her palm and pressed.

"Perhaps it was a bird."

The mirrored sea ribboned the ceiling of her hut. Anna-Maria sat upright again, looked at the horizon, and could not see a thing. "It must have been a boat," she thought, "sailing farther out."

She looked at the stone wall, but did not try to count. A piece of broken glass on top was a bright light.

"This early in the morning, stones cast a shadow," she thought, "the length of a body at least." She thought she might renew the rubble on the ground.

Anna-Maria decided to dress. She heard a sea gull cry. She thought of Panos Charaiambos and his shop, of how it looked in mornings, when she raised the blinds, of how it looked in evenings, when she needed light. She lifted her legs from the sheets and dropped them to the floor; she let her hair fall free. The floor was very cold.

"Today," she thought. "Today."

Still wearing her nightdress, she padded through the

door and out behind the house. She settled to her haunches, looking at the ground, pulling her nightdress high. She wondered when the first guests would arrive.

Behind the house, up on the hill, she saw the pit and the calf's body, turning, and the shepherd at the spit. He did not notice her. Brown smoke came from the pit; she heard the creaking of springs, of the great turning weight. She felt cold in the shadow of the house, stood up, and wandered back.

Anna-Maria made her bed, then, carefully, stepped to the wooden chest and opened it, selected a white dress.

"Today we celebrate," she thought. "Why not? There aren't so many times I get to wear this dress."

Stepping behind the screen, she took her night clothes off and got into her shift. She pulled on special stockings, white with a blue design, bright flowers and a vase. They felt too loose, too thick. She stood and stumbled, bent, sat heavily again. She fumbled with the buttons of her festive dress, could not arrange them, and decided, after all, to wait. "I should not wear this white one, not so early," she decided. "Not quite yet. It might get dirty with the breakfast, or with work. Later, I'll put it on." She folded it again, and set it on the chair. With ease, with habit and relief, she stepped into her black dress and belted tight the waist.

Anna-Maria crept back to her bed. Reaching beneath the mattress, on the right-hand side, she took her pouch of pipe tobacco, matches, and a pipe, then hurried out the door. Orsetta still lay quiet, on her back. "I will not have another chance today," Anna-Maria thought, filling the pipe and pushing the tobacco tightly down. "Someone would surely see."

When the doctors forbade Orsetta's smoking, Anna-Maria, too, had offered to give up her pipe, but this she could not do. She had thrown out the pipe in front of Orsetta, but, later, taking garbage to the pit, had fished it out again. Five and six times a day, when she could be alone, behind Orsetta's back, out on an errand or up in the hills, far from her sister's bed, she smoked a bowlful of tobacco, warm with the delight. If she could not escape, she would stand at the door, her white hair straggling loose, her thin hands crossed, clutching her dress, hiding the pipe, the matches, and the pouch, waiting till someone passed.

"What is the time?" she always asked. "Tell me the time"—bent forward, listening. And when the villager had made up time to tell her, pointing at the sun, she would half smile and nod, turn to Orsetta, say: "It's time to fetch the milk, to meet the schoolmaster."

Having explained herself, although it was a lie, although Orsetta often did not hear, Anna-Maria would go back behind the house and smoke, hidden from everyone, the smoke drifting with wind, would come to work again, only to say an hour later, standing in the door: "Please, what is the time?"

This was her single sin, and also, sometimes, to herself, she said that she was glad Orsetta could not smoke. The doctors had forbidden it, she said.

Apelis had discovered her, contented, by the beach, sucking at her pipe and waving smoke away. She had turned red with shame, but he had only laughed, and, afterwards, had brought her a tobacco tin. She never would have dared to ask for tobacco in the Charaki store, although she went there every day, although she had used up her old tobacco tins, so she relied upon Apelis' kindness, thanking him each night. Once he had brought her a great tin, two kilos of tobacco, too large to hide inside the house, so she had buried it, beneath a pile of weeds, for when she was outside.

And when, returning, sometimes, the smell still clung to her, when Orsetta was awake, and sniffed, and, watchful, asked her what was that, Anna-Maria had to answer: "Nothing, only wind."

At night, in her long prayers, kneeling by the bed and seeing, underneath the mattress, the place she kept her pipe, she would always commend Apelis and always ask mercy for her lies, saying that they were merciful, were meant to keep the calm. Now, as she lit up, delighted, secretive, settling behind the house, she told herself: "It's true. It is the wind that smells. Without the wind, there'd be no smell at all."

The sun was growing hot.

Stavros wiped off his face with a red handkerchief and tied it round his neck. He had spitted the calf, hard work for one man, heavy, inexact; and on loud springs it turned. The drippings of fat hissed. He saw Anna-Maria smoking out behind the house and wished he had a smoke.

Anna-Maria stood, and stretched, and went back to the house. She hid her pipe again. She started to prepare their breakfast, breathing softly, still tasting the smoke. She ate a piece of fruit. She wondered at how well Orsetta slept, how quietly. She could not hear a sound. A water jug in hand, she stepped toward the bed. Orsetta's eyes were open, and she did not make a sound.

Anna-Maria looked toward her bed, saw that the pipe was hidden, breathed again.

"Are you awake?" Anna-Maria asked. "It is a happy day."

"I'll give you your present," she thought, "before the others come."

Orsetta did not move nor sleep; she did not breathe at all.

Anna-Maria started to run from the house, to call Stavros for help. She dropped the water jug. It shattered on the floor, spattering water, clay. She could not leave Orsetta with her opened eyes. She spat upon her thumbs, rubbing them on the wet clay floor, the water and the porcelain, and closed her sister's eyelids, said: "Earth I have taken: you lie under earth."

"A man of Malona said to another: 'The thing that rises in the east, and that they call the sun, what is it?' 'The sun,' the other said. 'Somebody must have told you,' cried the first. 'No, no,' the second answered, 'as I hope to have joy from my mother.' "

Yannis laughed aloud. He shook his open hands. He told himself the story once again. He came out of the kitchen, called: "Hola, Apelis, answer this."

"All right," Apelis said, "but ask."

He waited by the wall. Soon it would be time. He had told only Vasilis, the gardener; Vasilis gathered grapes.

"No, no, I'll speak a riddle, and you answer me."

Apelis touched a vine. Soon Sotiris would come.

> *"The mountain sleeps in snow,*
> *the thick have thinned away;*
> *the little ones came near,*
> *and then the two were three,*
> *and all the friends I had*
> *are gone away and left."*

"I do not know," Apelis said. He heard the telephone.

"But guess," Yannis urged.

"I have to take the phone."

"An old man's song," Yannis announced. "It is an old man's song."

Apelis stepped inside.

Stavros was on the telephone and told Apelis of Orsetta's death. He had run to Malona to put through the call. The calf turned on the spit; now no one would eat meat. Apelis asked him when it had happened; Stavros did not know. He had left Anna-Maria crying in the house; she had not said a word, just pointed, rocking, then sat still. Apelis promised he would come, told Stavros to rush back to Charaki, to wait there. He called Andreas; Aliki answered. She said Andreas had just left to come to him; Apelis rang off. He wrote a note to Andreas that Orsetta was dead, that he should cancel all festivity and warn the guests not to go to Charaki, that he, Apelis, had gone there alone. Without telling the servants, leaving no other note, he got into his car and left.

Out on the empty road, he realized he had forgotten to

tell Andreas that Sotiris would come, and chose to go himself, to the airport, afterwards.

Andreas, wearing a white shirt and linen jacket, sandals and a tie, walked into the garden, saw Vasilis, the gardener, and, smiling, crossed to him. Vasilis, having picked the grapes, had stooped to pull out weeds and small shoots from the topsoil of the vines.

"You are here early, sir," he said.

"Early, why so? It is past ten o'clock."

"Yes, yes, but they are not expected until three."

"Well, then, they will be late," Andreas said, not listening, his hand upon a rake. "The party starts at one."

"Your father has just left."

"And when will he be back?"

"Now that I cannot say—but soon he will go to the airport, will be back at three. Or possibly go straight to Charaki, and not return. I cannot say."

"The airport, why?" Andreas turned his head.

Vasilis plucked a weed. "You do not know?" he asked.

"To meet the king of Greece."

"Éla, you truly do not know?"

"To meet the one bishop of Crete." Andreas wiped his face.

"Your brother will return."

"Now it is you who joke."

"I tell you truly, he is here."

"You joke," Andreas said.

"May I not see the dawn if it is not the truth." Vasilis raised his arm. "May I spit on the shrine of a saint. He called this morning, early, and will take the plane. He shall be here at three. He called at six o'clock—your father answered it. Your father has been waiting. He will bring him home."

Andreas walked away, walked round the garden, came completely back, picked up the bunch of grapes and threw them at the wall. They crumpled and they burst. Inside, he found the note, propped up beside the telephone, not that Sotiris would arrive, but that Orsetta was dead.

Time passed, the morning and the early afternoon; Apelis stayed near to his mother's house. He met the priests, arranged for washing and the services, spoke to Anna-Maria, who would not answer a word, and gave Stavros the calf. It would need to be cooked, but could not be eaten. Andreas, in Apelis' home, called all invited guests, saying they should not go to Charaki, that Orsetta was dead. No one was unprepared; nobody found a will. One man, however, a jeweller, had already departed; Andreas could not reach him, and, miscalculating time, the jeweller drove to Charaki, met Apelis on the wooden walk, and said, embracing him: "Congratulations: may she long survive."

HIS THIN FACE black with sun, with dirt, his long hair curling down, his clothes encrusted, old, Sotiris stepped from the airplane to see Apelis waiting. He held onto the guard rail, walking down, and watched his father's face. Apelis, standing straight, half lifted his right hand. Sotiris stepped onto the concrete ground; his father took his arm. "I have no bags," Sotiris said. "We can already go." They walked out to the car.

Apelis had stood sentinel by Orsetta's death bed; Anna-Maria wept. Heat blanketed the room. The shutters and the door stood closed; he burned sticks of incense. The smell was very strong; Orsetta lay unwashed. He walked outside, in sun, with priests, and to talk to Stavros. He went up to the pit. Anna-Maria stayed, her flowered legs splayed out. He had wept by her side.

"Orsetta died last night."

"Last night!" Sotiris turned.

"Late last night, or this morning. I've just come from there."

Anna-Maria's festival stockings had fallen to her ankles and hung loose.

The road was free of cars.

"She was in Charaki, still. This morning, when we spoke, I had not yet been told."

Small clouds patterned the sky. Aliki changed her dress.

"This afternoon," Sotiris said, "was to have been her feast."

Returning from America, Apelis had been met, at the harbour, by Orsetta, had been a false hero returned and carried flowers home.

"I hope she had no pain. They couldn't tell me when she died, or how."

"When will they have the funeral?"

"Tomorrow, in Malona, in the afternoon."

"Anna-Maria, how is she?"

"Alone," Apelis said.

Orsetta had been welcoming, had never understood. Apelis wondered what his son had seen.

"This morning, when we spoke, I thought her still alive."

Sotiris counted trees.

"I thought you hurt, or lost somewhere. I am glad you have come."

Silent, they reached the house; Andreas was not there. He, too, had left a note, propped up beside the phone, saying that he was gone, that everything was done. This evening the first mourners would arrive.

"Get out of those clothes," said Apelis. "Go up to your room. Clean yourself, come down again, and I'll have you some food. You must be hungry."

Sotiris greeted servants; they all were wearing black. Andreas would have ordered it, and would wear black himself.

Three flights of stairs he climbed and turned into his room. The room was all unchanged; he lay down on the bed.

Pulling out a guitar, he opened up the case. The top two strings had snapped and curled up to the neck; the wood was grey with dust. He placed it on the bed.

He went into the bathroom, took his old clothes off, and shed them in a pile. In the light, in the mirror, he saw the line of dirt like rope around his neck, the bracelets at his feet; he stepped into the shower, scraped his body down.

> *On mountains the thistle grows,*
> *your words were honey.*

He wondered, could he weep? In September sun that broke the bathroom window like a blade, he dried himself, walked naked to his room. Opening the sweet-scented chest, he selected clothing and put shoes upon his feet. Hungry, wearing black, he hurried down the stairs.

Apelis waited at the stair foot, said: "She gave this to me, yesterday. For you," and placed within his hand a silver ring.

Fat, fallen-breasted, and inert, Aliki would be soon; he knew it: he could see. She looped her hair in front of the mirror, brown-yellow hair, and did not turn around.

Andreas sat down on the bed. "Sotiris has returned," he said. "My father never told."

She turned to stare at him. He smiled and did not speak.

Sotiris, with Apelis watching, ate a bowl of soup and started eating fish. A cook brought in a bowl of white potatoes, covered with a sauce. Sotiris fell asleep. Apelis took a pillow, placed it carefully beneath his head and closed the doors, walked out.

White, witless and directional, the water in the warm sea flowed, the crowd went walking up and down—the night had fully come. Sunset was slow and clear, a parting long prolonged. Sotiris, in the garden, met his family. In turn, and changing colour with the sun, they spoke to him of sorrow, of the welcome home. Andreas and Aliki had arrived; Andreas had been distant, Aliki too loud. "We heard you were asleep," she said. "Did you sleep well?"

Manos and Eleni, Yannis, Apelis' servants, friends, the far-off relatives and mourners of the waiting room filed past. Apelis spoke with them, and offered each a glass of raki and dried figs. Noiseless, they hovered, slapping palm on palm; Sotiris slipped away.

Wounds, wounds you make of my body,
give me the herb that heals.

He walked to Dania's house.

Yannis and Aliki stood together in Apelis' kitchen, con-sidering the food. Three cooks had passed the week pre-paring it for Orsetta's feast day, but now the celebration food was to be used for mourning, condolence visitors, and the next day's condolence meal.

A soft, circular moon shone in a goat's belly sky. He touched the walls of streets.

"Hello," Chrysanthi said.
"Embrós. Enter."
She wore a pleated dress. Phillipos did not look.
"I am not late?" she said.

"Not very, no one else is here."

Yannis spent much time in the kitchen, had nearly lived there the last week, was a good cook and taster; now he played the guide. Having already taken home the celebration cakes, he showed Aliki what was left for use.

Phillipos raised his head, saw her before him, in the half-light, said:
"What, have you come alone?"
"Why, yes," she said, and kissed him. "Yes, alone."

He came to Dania's house and waited in the shadows, looking up, not wanting to rush in. He thought he saw her move against a window, saw that she moved without rest, and realized she was a tree reflected by the moon. Far off, in a far street, a woman sang. He heard it in the wind.

> *Let us go where you say,*
> *where the birds make their nest.*

Pointing toward the plates, the bowls and high-heaped trays, Yannis announced: "We have a lot of food."

Moving up to the wall, he saw Mehmet Effendi lying back, asleep, in his great chair. The room was dark, the house, dark, the outside, where he stood, moonlit; he had the sudden fear that she might see him first.

"Psarózoumo, fish broth; soúpa fakí, made of lentil," Yannis said. "Barboúnia, red mullet; grilled and garlic-covered eel."

"At last, I have you here again."
And Phillipos arose.
"At last, what do you mean?" Chrysanthi asked. "I came here yesterday."
"But not alone. With company: your dear distracted love."

"I know," Aliki said. "I am a cook also."

Sotiris scrabbled in the courtyard after pebbles, threw some at her window, but soon stopped. He knelt down by the window, waiting, faintly heard Mehmet Effendi snore, knelt there until his legs grew stiff, giving no balance, stood again. He chose to go inside.

"The night before was the last time that you came here alone. Two nights, two nights entire." And he smiled. "What do you think I am? Take off your clothes."
He locked the door.
Chrysanthi laughed. "The others will be coming soon."
"We have enough time. Here."
"Then hurry."

"Hurry. Here."

She would be careful. He was drunk.

"We have to rush," she said.

Phillipos walked across the room, adjusting lights, then went back to the door, unfastened it.

"If they should come," he said, "as it's to be a party, we will allow them to watch."

"I know," Aliki said. "I helped preparing, too."

Manos and Eleni walked together from Apelis' house.

The door squeaked slightly, though he lifted as he pushed, and it gave without resistance. Mehmet Effendi slept. He saw there was no light on in the kitchen, held his breath and went straight up the stairs, keeping closely to the inside edge where they would creak less, spacing steps to coincide with the old Turk's snores. He reached the landing, listened, readying himself, then opened the door to her room.

When Phillipos returned, Chrysanthi lay there naked, restless, watching him, supported on a pillow, clothes upon the floor. He stood above her, distant, looking down, taking his own clothes off and adding to the pile, then, stripped, lay next to her and took her mouth in his.

"Imagine," Manos said, "how it would be if Triphon were to come. The three brothers together once again."

"Two are enough," Eleni said.

Anna-Maria slept.

Sotiris felt his stomach loosen, recognized Dania, before
him, in a chair. The bells rang nine o'clock, and then she
noticed him.

Incense burned by the bed. Anna-Maria wore her stockings; she held on to her pipe.

> *You are the flower of flowers,*
> *the scented hyacinth;*
> *you were born*
> *together with the sun.*

Sotiris stepped inside.
She wore a yellow dress.
"I'm back," Sotiris said. "I came this afternoon."
"I never knew that you were coming back."
"I did not know myself."
"How are you?" Dania asked, and sat up on the chair.
"Orsetta died," he said. "My grandmother."
"Oh, I am sorry, sorry. When?"
"Late y-yesterday, they say, without much pain. Today
was to have been her festival."
"Yes, she was very ill. I am so sorry," Dania said.

Chrysanthi touched his legs.

"The funny thing is"—and Yannis smiled—"that we

should be this ready with the food. Much better this way
than to have to make it all"—he snapped his fingers—"at
a moment's notice, just like that."

She was a girl gone far away; Sotiris could not speak. He
looked at the wood carving on the wall.

> *I bring you lemons, lady,*
> *that you may make love.*

"And you, how are you now?" he asked.
"When will they have the funeral?"
"Tomorrow. How are you?"
"What makes you ask?" she said.
The room was very cold.
"What do you mean?"
"Did you return because she died?"
"Part of the reason, yes. I hoped she would still be
alive."
"She had been very ill."

"Of course," Yannis considered, "we still shall have to
make the kólliva. And that takes work," he said.

Chrysanthi started to respond and wrapped her hands
around his back, but he sat suddenly erect again, reached
for the pile of clothes, and threw them far across the room.
"Just so you will not think that we can stop in time,"

Phillipos said, and, smiling, looked at scattered colour, walls, and at her face.

Anna-Maria slept a dreamless sleep, drugged, lying on her left side. A squirrel ran into the chimney, scampered back again; she heard nothing at all.

"Are you all right?" Sotiris said.
"I am just tired, thank you very much." And Dania stretched.
"But you know what I mean?"
"No, truly, what is it you mean?"
"How do you feel?" he said.
"Why should you care?"
He heard Mehmet Effendi snore. "I care," he said. "I care."

"I stood in the long rain and waited for you," Phillipos sang. "But, ah, you were untrue—and left me with wet feet."

"Broiled langouste bits and shrimp." Aliki tasted one. "Fried mussels, octopus and marinated octopus, fried squid, and psitó boúti, six roast legs of lamb. But those we cannot use. The waste of all this meat."

"I care," Sotiris said again. "I do."
"In that case, I am wonderful. Oh, everything is wonderful."

"Don't be that way," Sotiris said. "Please, come out for a walk."

"I tell you I am tired."

"I have come," he said, "to stay."

"Then welcome home."

He wanted now to laugh. "Behave yourself," he said.

And he saw that she was crying, heard her cry: "Just go!"

The door had opened, softly, and then stopped. Chrysanthi, looking up, over his dipping shoulder, looking out across the room, saw shapes of three people, two men and a girl. She cleared her head: Kostas, Alexandra, and Phokion. Phillipos, too, had turned, half risen on his hands, and called:

"Come in. We were expecting you. Sit down, we will be finished soon."

He pleaded with her still, and she agreed to come out for a walk. She put a sweater on, a white one he had never seen, and threaded soft white sandals to her feet. They opened the door, went down creaking stairs, not speaking, carefully, passed Mehmet Effendi, and were both outside.

"I'll go to the café," Manos decided, "after this, when she's asleep, tonight."

Phokion had opened Alexandra's blouse, and bending her back, poured wine on her stomach, licked it off. Phillipos did the same. He crossed then to Chrysanthi, poured some wine upon her, fingered it and sucked his fingers, whistled at the taste. She, too, was growing drunk. She laughed and turned away.

Yannis plucked a fig and started peeling it.

"Tomorrow," thought Sotiris, "I will try again."

Chrysanthi counted flowers on the wall.

The sky was clear, the buildings close and secret-seeming; soon it would be fall. Walking with her, he felt each motion of his leg, wished she could feel them too; the flexing and release of muscle, balancing of weight. He did not take her hand.

"Dolmádes, rice in vine leaves; small keftédes, baby meatballs of ground lamb, seasoned with dill"—Yannis pointed—"feta, the goat's cheese, mushroom, egg."

They walked in silence through the warrens of the Old Town, out above the harbour and the small caïques, above a pile of langouste pots and smell of sewage hanging in the air. An old man, in the distance, checked his nets. He waved, Sotiris answered, and they turned away.

"I wonder who will eat it all," Aliki said.
"Ah, the entire village"—and Yannis nodded wisely—"will be here. Myself, I like the figs."

"But there is so much food," she muttered, "even without meat."

Rounding a curve in the low wall and coming into wind, they lost the light of the fisherman's blue lantern, and the city lights; there, on a sloping rock, they sat together, quiet, looking at the sea.

"But twenty people," said Yannis, "hungry ones, mind you, like those of the village, could manage all of this."

Manos wondered if Triphon had been told, if he would soon arrive.

In front of him, Sotiris saw an old crate and a dead tree, a newspaper in shaling stone. He got up, felt the salt spray coming in a gust and knew they would be wet, but gathered them together, broke the crate and branches off the tree, made a small fire in the land side of the rock. They sat in front of it, out of the wind, watching the damp wood smoulder, burn, wondering what to say.

> *The eyes of my love*
> *are not very large;*
> *they are as sweet as honey,*
> *black as ink.*
> *My heart has four leaves;*
> *two you have already burnt,*
> *the other two you leave*
> *all withered, all in black.*

Kostas stood looking down and pulled a bracelet from his pocket, gold and silver intertwined, a patterning of snakes. He gave it to Chrysanthi, smiled, and then, when she had seen it, took it back. He showed it round the room and said: "Chrysanthi, this is yours." She still lay on the bed, covered only by sheets, with one leg hanging loose.

"On this condition, this single condition: that you let me give it you in my desired way." He winked.

"I am in love with you," Sotiris said, looking down at his feet, "far more than I have ever known or wanted to admit. I cannot tell you even now how much you mean to me; I do not know myself. I am in love with you."

Phillipos sat upon the floor, holding his spread knees. She answered yes, and Kostas took his pants off, wearing nothing underneath, and threw his pants to Alexandra, kept his shoes and socks. He sat down on the bed, in view of the others, excited, touched Chrysanthi, then circled himself with the thick, sharp-sided braclet, and, balancing carefully, he entered into her. Phokion and Alexandra looked away. "You're hurting me," Chrysanthi cried out once: "Aieee!" when he became too rough and the bracelet dug too deep, but soon he satisfied himself and rolled away from her, the red welts rising quickly on his skin.

"It's yours," he said. "It's yours."

"I cannot give a name to what is you, perhaps there are no words, perhaps I have not learned them yet, perhaps I never will. The loneliness of cities is far worse than loneliness of land," Sotiris said, "and harder far to bear."

The bells rang ten o'clock. And Signor Smith, listening, laughed. The wood was entirely his.

Yannis pointed to the window. "Over there," he said, "various wines, bread, biscuits, and the fruit."

> *Woman in the field,*
> *cut for me, too, pomegranates.*

Apelis and Andreas stood outside; the guests had all gone home.
"You didn't tell me he would come," Andreas said.
"I was too hurried, leaving, and forgot."
"I should have liked to know. I had the right to know."
"Well, anyway, he came."

"I could not walk the city streets, watching the pretty couples pass, or girls reminding me of you, or parties, people, anyone, without remembering and wanting something more. Something that I once had."

Chrysanthi touched the flowers on the wall.

"What people," Alexandra thought. "Kostas, especially."

"Sometimes the opposite," Sotiris said. "I joined a party,

stayed with it, upon the outside, more or less, but still a little less alone."

Anna-Maria slept and would sleep until day, the candles burning by her side, above her sister's head, dreaming no dream at all.

Dania remembered, for no reason, an old song. She tried to listen, tried to pay attention, but the words he spoke were the words of her song.

"What all the others strive to do," Sotiris said, "you have no need of, need not even try. What all the others imitate, you are, unknowing, with no smallest effort, from the start."

"The start," she heard, and, quiet, sang:
> *"Oh, my second thought,*
> *why were you not the first?*
> *Why did you not construct,*
> *why did you not provide*
> *an iron door,*
> *a door of steel*
> *to put across my heart?"*

He tried to, could not, tell her of Chrysanthi, and fell silent, wondering.

"You have your bracelet, and you are not satisfied," Phillipos said. "Come, come."

"Yaoúrti, velvet cake, halva, sweetmeats, and baklavá and, here, a rose-leaf spread."

"Not that I am angry, understand," Andreas said, "not that, only a little hurt."

"Of course you are angry," Apelis said, "but, nonetheless, he came."

Sotiris poked the fire, realized it would take time before he had the faith to tell her, the trust she would listen and hear, the faith he would know what to say—and knew then, bitterly, how little of her he yet knew.

"A man can understand," Manos repeated, "everything you think."

The small fire grew great and settled, cowering, again. Sotiris felt his leg.

"Sotiris," Dania said.

"Yes?"

". . . to put across my heart," she thought.

"Nothing; only Sotiris."

Every time she spoke his name, he took it as a gift, a small surprise, an offering.

"I want you very much," he said.

She made no answer, looked at him. He willed himself content.

"Phillipos!" Holding her bracelet, from the bed, she cried.

"Chrysanthi, nai, what is it, yes?"

He held a bottle in his hand, stood over her.

"Today Sotiris left."

He could go back to Athens, go back in the morning, never tell her how she made him leave. Perhaps, he thought, it would be best.

"Oréa," Phillipos replied. "How nice. Now have a drink."

Where had she got that sweater? Who had given it? Why had she been up in her room, alone?

"The kokorétsi, entrails out of lamb."

"You do not understand," Chrysanthi said. "He left this morning, or last night. The only thing that he could find to say was 'I am gone.'"

"It was too far to go," Sotiris said. She stiffened; there beside him, in the dark, he saw. "You have forgotten me."

Where had she got that sweater? Who had given it? Tell nothing and learn nothing, he said to himself, this stranger by my side.

"You have forgotten me," he said, and wondered was it true.

"He called me by a final name. 'Chryso,' he used to say."

"Yes, yes," Manos decided, "afterwards, I'll go to the café. I'll stay the whole night through."

"Now sit up, please, and have another drink. It's no great loss," Phillipos said.
"I want no more; just go."

"And will he really come tomorrow?" Dania thought. "The next day, and the next?"

"I grew so sick of life in that hellhole," he said.

"The kourambiédes, little cakes; pastítsio, a macaroni pie."

He could have sung, have said thanks to the sky. For finally she turned to him and asked:
"You have come back to me?"
And Dania took his hand.
"You will not leave me for a while, not run away again?"
"I have come home to stay."
"Not for the week at least—you will give us a little time together, only that. I told myself I would not ask it, and you need not answer, but I need a little time. It's been so very long."
"This stranger by my side," he thought.
"I have come home to stay."

A single sea bird called.

"And if I go," he said, "you will go with me where I go."

Chrysanthi turned away from him, her body sticky with the wine, her legs and arms drawn close together, bracelet in her hand.

"Be nice," he said, and shifted balance. "Have another drink."

> *Let us go where you say,*
> *where the birds make their nest.*

Sotiris rose to leave, took the small sticks of wood, the glowing branches of the tree by their still untouched ends, and, one by one, he whirled them down along the rocks and out to sea, rainbows of fire, crimson, flaring up, brands catapulted to the sea and scattered charcoal stars. She watched him bend and straighten, lit with mirrored glow, then swing his arms and stand in darkness, time and time again, the pinwheels flickering, hot hissing at the sea, and knew she never would forget these moments and this joy.

He stood above her, drinking off the wine, then turned her flat upon her back and offered her a drink. When she did not accept, he shook his shoulders, finished it himself. And, thoughtful, looking down, he placed the bottle carefully between her legs, the last drops running out, nose down, his hand around the base, inserted it, and pushed.

HE TOLD HER OF CHRYSANTHI, truly, after all, and at the very end. They walked together, back to Dania's house, his arm around her shoulders, and her hand upon his neck. She had been very gentle, near; he felt himself unclean. He kissed her in the courtyard, but, as she turned to go, he called her back. "Stay, Dania," he had asked, after telling her of Phillipos, Athens, the long, total story of his time away and all it meant to him, what he had slowly learned, not asking her forgiveness, and leaving nothing out. She stood, a pillar, crying, by the door. "I tried not to believe it," Dania said. "I tried so very hard. Don't spoil it now, don't tell me any more" —and turned from him to go inside her house.

"There's nothing more to tell," he said into the door. He loved her, and he loved the town; he walked home slowly, reverent. A low light burned still in the patio; he saw the servants washing tables and arranging chairs. Mute, they moved in silence, did not notice him. Inside the study, sitting alone, he saw his father looking at the wall. A single, white light shone; the clock showed nearly twelve. Apelis did not turn or hear, and he waited a minute, looking at his father's face, the heavy chiselled head and eyes made hollow by the dark, the sinews of the neck and starting folds of age.

Apelis turned to see him, pushed a telegram across the table, and Sotiris read:

MOST DEEPLY SHOCKED AM COMING STOP FORBID MY THIRD OF HOUSE BE ENTERED STOP MAYOR RETAIN POSSESSION MUST OF KEY STOP EVERYTHING KEEP LEGAL STOP CONDOLENCES TO ALL STOP FLY TOMORROW LAWYER TOO TRIPHON.

"What do you think of it?" his father asked.

He read it once again:

MOST DEEPLY SHOCKED AM COMING STOP FORBID MY THIRD OF HOUSE BE ENTERED STOP MAYOR RETAIN POSSESSION MUST OF KEY STOP EVERYTHING KEEP LEGAL STOP CONDOLENCES TO ALL STOP FLY TOMORROW LAWYER TOO TRIPHON.

Apelis waited for an answer, but Sotiris merely knew the question: what did all this mean?

"We shall have legal troubles, too," his father said. "As if it weren't enough."

"It seems we'll have to wait," Sotiris said.

"Yes, it appears so. I am sorry, too."

"Well I, for one, can wait."

Apelis looked away. He turned an ash tray round and round, rubbing his finger in ash.

"I saw your grandmother last night, late yesterday, a little while before she died."

"When she gave you the ring?"

"When she gave me the ring. She also said"—Apelis looked at him—"that she had lied to you."

"Go out to Charaki," he thought, "and tell them I shall swim."

"How do you mean, she lied?"

"She did not tell you the true treasure spot," Apelis said.

"Then take some tools inside a towel, tell everyone to leave. Go in the room," he thought, "and see."

"She didn't tell it to me either," his father said. "She wanted it for you, and meant it to be yours, but then you went away."

"Break down the door tomorrow night," he thought, "when the village sleeps, and dig."

"Then nobody will know," Sotiris said.

"She would have told you, had you come again."

"Perhaps there is no treasure, nothing left at all," Sotiris said. "Perhaps three thousand drachmas was the lot."

"I thought that I should tell you, so you would not hope too much nor be too disappointed with this wait."

"And truly I don't care," Sotiris told himself, "if it exists at all."

A fretless oúda, played above the head, will turn musicians blindly, lead them toward light.

Sotiris followed scales to silence, chose the footless, wing as crutch, and found himself resolved.

"But is it possible she lied," he asked, "at the end? Or did not know herself where it really was—that, earlier, she told the truth?"

"Yes, that may be," Apelis said. "We will just have to wait. Now that the lawyers come. . . ."

"But that she lied to me," Sotiris thought, and touched the telegram.

"The money, if she lied, is yours."

"I have two brothers, also," Apelis replied, "and there was no will. Nothing we know of, at least. Just like Orsetta, isn't it, to leave no will, to let us argue, fight, to bring the lawyers in. Mitéramou." Apelis hung his head.

"The money, if she lied to me, is yours. Before I left, we had agreed, and that agreement stays."

"We can know nothing yet. Perhaps we never shall. And, you know"—Apelis smiled at him—"I doubt if Manos and Triphon would easily agree."

"It's not important, I no longer care. You ought to get some sleep," Sotiris said. "I slept this afternoon."

Sotiris went to his room, took his clothes off, and laid them on a chair; he heard the servants moving down below. His father called good night. In bed, he stretched to feel the clean sheets cold against his skin, turned over once, and slept.

WITH GROUND CORN boiled in water and pine kernels mixed in, with flour baked brown, the kólliva was made. Old women added sugar, cinnamon, and, on a special silver dish, walnuts. Orderly, they added almonds placed along the edge, and, alternating, out of sugared almonds, in the center, wrapped in silver and gold leaf, they wrote the name Orsetta. Hung beads drive Signor Smith away; they wore blue at the neck. Embroidering, well-spaced, they strewed the sugared flowers round, and left their kitchen, late.

Sotiris was aroused with dawn; he tried to fall asleep again, could not. He dressed himself, went softly down the stairs; it was a house in black. He went into the kitchen, twisted free a great handful of grapes, threw on an old coat, and walked quietly outside. He wandered to the harbour, chilled by the unbroken wind, huddled in his sheepskin, and finishing the grapes. He watched the sun rise in the harbour, on the fishing boats, and climbed out, sat in one of them, watching the sky and sea wash into orange, his own flaming face in the water below; with wind quite loud upon the shore, the boat rocked in the swell.

Still cold, wrapped in his coat, his sandals wet with dew, he climbed back to the dock and walked past empty cafés to the small Turkish graveyard, Murad Reis. The summer took possession of the sky. Inside, he sat upon the earth, smelling the mulberry and oleander, the great baobab, and looking at stones, the turbaned tombs and vaults, hearing no sound but wind.

> *You sleep in the sheets,*
> *and I walk about;*
> *you sleep with your candle still lit,*
> *I walk about;*
> *you sleep in the mosquito net,*
> *I walk about;*
> *you sleep in the white sheets,*
> *I walk about in snow.*

Inside the house, his father and his brother were awake. Apelis had summoned Andreas for breakfast; the two of them sat at the head of the long dining table, alone. They both were dressed in black. Sotiris walked in to join them; no one else was up.

"Triphon arrives this afternoon. Today the lawyers come."

"And on her funeral."

"The mayor of Malona will be there, keeping an eye

out for Triphon, for priests. And Panayotis, too, the one Triphon has bought."

"The house will be padlocked."

He felt warmed in the house; wet grass was on his feet.

"Sotis, what will you have to eat? You were not in your room."

"No, I walked to the harbour, and to Murad Reis. I saw the dawn."

"I, too," his father said. "I couldn't sleep."

"Today will be a long day—yesterday was long," Andreas said. "It would have been better to sleep."

"Sotiris, you should eat."

Andreas buttered bread and served him with some eggs. They ate together, the three men, picking at the food.

"The funeral will be at two."

"And when do we go to Charaki?" Sotiris asked.

"We cannot go till one."

And they decided that Sotiris would go to Ioannidis, the casket maker, arrange for delivery of the coffin, and have it sent to Charaki. Apelis had spoken with him the day before; the coffin was complete. Sotiris would make sure, would drive to the village, alone, and supervise the laying out of Orsetta. Depending on how quickly they could come, he would wait for the others at Charaki, or at the village church. Apelis and Andreas would have to spend the morning with the lawyers, making ready for Triphon and the condolence feast, receive the kólliva. The service was to be outside Malona, at exactly two.

Andreas took the plates and glasses from the table, started to the kitchen, but returned. Holding the plates, he crossed to where his brother sat and looked down at him, at the tired face, the little lines under his eyes, the high cheekbones and way he held his head.

"I am glad you are back."

Apelis rose also.

"He has come back, Mehmet."

Mehmet Effendi turned; he wore his yellow fez.

"He has come back again."

They were at work upon a chair; he held it steady, out, while she measured the bottom, checking distances. Dania would cover it with cloth; she had to know how much.

"Who has come back?" he said. He set the chair down flat.

"Can you not guess?" she asked. She shook her long hair free.

"The Sultan," he said, hoping it was true. "The Sultan, whom I met in Egypt once, who was in prison there."

Dania did not reply.

"The Sultan has come back."

She wore a purple shirt.

"Who is it, then?" he asked. He fingered the straw chair. He rubbed his foot on straw.

"You must not be afraid," she said.

"Afraid, what do you mean?"

"I mean you must not mind," she said, and smiled to comfort him.

Mehmet Effendi stared. He gathered up his pipe. He lit the pipe, but there was no tobacco in the bowl; he had forgotten it. He sucked in flame, and coughed.

"Sotiris has come back."

"The Sultan," he replied, "I met in Egypt once, who was in prison there."

"Sotiris," Dania said. "You do remember him."

"The doctor," Mehmet said, his eyes gone wide with fear. "The one who helped you with your arm, the one who helped my leg. He has come back again."

"Sotiris," Dania said.

He looked around the room. "The one with the carpet," he offered, "who has flown away."

"That carpet brought him back."

He hid his match from sight, inside his shirt pocket. He hoped it would not show. "He ought not to come here."

"You need not be afraid."

"The one with the carpet," Mehmet Effendi said.

"He has returned to me."

Dressed, he drove past the flowering gardens and gullies of the castle wall to Ioannidis, the casket maker's shop, in a little square. The shop was closed. Under a plane tree, kittens played with bits of string; the mother cat half slept. From Ioannidis' house, he heard the sounds of women, saw them look at him. He pushed at the shop door, it gave, he walked into the dark workroom. There Ioannidis stood, his great arms sawdust-whitened, folded on his chest.

"Yásou," Sotiris said.

"Yásou, and welcome back."

"How does it go?" Sotiris asked.

"My work"—he spat—"my work."

He spat again. He held a flask of linseed oil cradled in his hand; he closed the open door.

"How is your family?" Sotiris said.

"Well, they are always well. And yours?"

He tapped the linseed oil.

Ioannidis had six sisters, each of them ugly, all of them stupid, the youngest, twenty-nine. He wanted to marry them off, but could not, and had never grown resigned. Once, a butcher had offered to marry the youngest, if Ioannidis would buy him a shop, but Ioannidis could not afford the dowry, and the elder sisters would not allow him to try; so all the sisters stayed unmarried, hating each other, hating him.

He had been a good carpenter, and a careful man; in addition to caskets, he built fine doors for the New Town hotels and houses; he made furniture repairs, and sometimes carved small figures from a block. These he would never sell. Sometimes, when working on his coffins, he thought, if he could only nail a sister underneath, then everything would be much easier for him. And if a sister came upon him in that mood, came to complain about the other women, or of some night noise, or to him, Ioannidis, that he did not earn enough, he would turn to the sister, smiling, which she could not understand.

For ten years, ever since his father died, he had been the single man to step inside the house. The butcher never came inside; they had no relatives, the house was very calm. Once every month, however, Ioannidis would go to the workroom at night and drink the whole night through,

would come the next day in to breakfast, roaring, pounding the table, scattering sawdust and oil, demanding service, swearing that he would soon marry and leave the
sisters to go on the street. But they were not afraid; they
searched the Old Town for a candidate and could find
none; he had grown bald and dirty.

"No one else would have you," the sisters cackled, hating him.

And Ioannidis hung his head, played with his fork, and
smiled.

He had a secret love. The sisters never guessed.

He often walked along the beach to hunt for wood, and,
on the beach one day, washed up or dumped from off a
boat, he found the top part of a wooden woman, carved
down to her thighs. Waterlogged, an imitation goddess,
covered with long hair, it still had colour, naked, smelling
of the sea. He covered it with sand.

That night, in secret, Ioannidis drove his truck out to
the beach, as near as possible to the wet wooden figure-
head he'd found. He fashioned levers out of logs, and,
working hard, for she was heavy, hoisted her up to the
seat. Again, in secret, he carried her home, into the workshop, hiding her, as he could think of no more perfect
place, in a great oaken coffin he was finishing.

Night after night, and, in the days, when he was sure
of privacy, a market day, or Sunday, when his sisters had
filed off to church, he laboured at the wooden woman,
making her complete. Whittling and polishing, he pared
her lines down subtly, opened a long space in her long
hair so he could see her breast, carved "Ioannidis" on her

back, and "Love me always, I" upon her thigh. He fashioned balsa legs, using the light wood so they would be pliable, attached them to the bottom of the thighs, joined each with loose joints at the knee, and drilled a wide, white hole down through her stomach to the back.

It started, he would tell himself, as fun, but slowly it grew into love, this joy he took in his wooden woman. Unlike the sisters, she could move just when he willed it, could not speak, was always beautiful and hard. He finished the oak coffin, rubbed soft oils upon her body, lined the case with felt, and, whittling his small figures, threw them in to keep her company, to be her children and his sons. Then, once a month, at night, he would lock all the entrance doors, bring out a bottle of ouzo, and take her on the table, surround her with children, and talk. "Rectitude," he said, "and respect. I commend you for silence, command." All of his philosophy he offered to her then. "The reason we are here tonight is no reason, is unreason," he said. One of the whittled figures was a girl, and her Ioannidis would scold. "You and your skirt tails," he cried, "will trouble me all of my time. Take care, or I'll cut them away!" Then, in the mornings, still drunk, still argumentative, he would sit at the table with his sisters, prophetlike and loud, insisting he would marry and they could go to the streets.

Lately, however, he had felt the need far more than once a month, the need for solace and talk, and often in the nights he would sneak to his workshop, touch her cold and well-oiled body, carve his name upon her newly, or give a new figure as gift. His business declined. He no longer made wooden doors; he fell behind with coffins, often was too late. Sometimes, even, in the afternoons, when the longing grew too powerful, when the silence from her corner filled and became song, he would close up the shop and warn his sisters not to let him be disturbed, would double lock the doors and turn with relief to the one coffin he could never sell, the woman that was his.

And, on this morning, when Sotiris came, he had just turned to it, just chosen to be buried in the coffin, when his time came, with his obedient love. He listened to her thanks; he graciously said: "Stay." So he was angry and embarrassed when Sotiris spoke.

"My grandmother's coffin?" Sotiris said.

"Your grandmother, my sister." Ioannidis spat.

"It's ready, I hope."

"I who make it, sell it," said Ioannidis. "You who buy it, do not use it, and she who uses it has no further need."

Sotiris did not smile.

"You should have bought it ready made. Yes, yes." And Ioannidis said: "You will pay now, or when?"

He did not care; he half turned to the side.

The lovely colour of her skin, the way she came to him from water, lying in the sand, his first nights with her, conversations held, the way she bore his markings, name, and never would resist; all of this, this poetry, he would soon have to tell. One morning, soon, one of these days, he would bring all his sisters to the shop and line them up in front of the oak chest, then open it, explain, and introduce his love, install her in the house. They could go on the streets; he wanted them to know.

"I'll bring it," he said, "out to Charaki, in the truck. Don't worry," he said, "I shall be glad to come."

Sotiris stayed to finish the arrangements, paid, and left. Ioannidis turned back.

"Already," he announced, "they treat me like a thief. And she but newly dead. It's rectitude," Ioannidis said, "that makes for my respect. My treasure," he said to the wall, "in all unreason, you."

Sotiris did not turn off for Charaki: taking the next road, he drove to the sea. The metal windmills turned with wind, sailless and silent, treadmills for a mouse. And owls secreted perfect skeletons of mice and dropped them on the stone. He walked down to the sea.

There, standing on dry rock, he took his clothes off, laid them carefully on grass, the tie and the black suit, the heavy leather shoes, and walked into the water, swam out into the bay. Nearly a half mile out, he turned to see Charaki clustered in the center of the bay, pavilion of the sea, some small white houses and a stretch of beach; he saw Orsetta's house. The water was still warm; he swam back to the shore. Near rocks, he dove and searched the shelfing, saw a langouste scuttle back to hide. He surfaced, breathed, and went to search again; the langouste hid beneath a rock, antennae waving. Sotiris rose again and dove, expelled air at the langouste, waved his hands to ripple the water; the langouste backed away. Sotiris reached behind it, took hold from the rear. Waving its great tail helplessly, it surfaced under him. He took it, dark green, limp-shelled still from shedding, to the rocks and set it down on shore. It scuttled clumsily and fell upon its back, convulsive, tail slapping at rock. Thinking of the last time he had fished near Charaki, of the sea he had crossed twice but would not need to again, he picked it up, curved it inward from the tail, and threw it to the sea. It sank.

He dried himself in sun, seeing his silhouette wave with the water, and, dressed, returned to the car.

"A man of Malona," Manos said to his wife, "saw the moon in his oil jar and thought it was a thief. He took an axe and smashed the jar, hoping to catch the thief. The oil spilled out; the man slipped on it, thought it was the thief again who caught him by the foot. 'Don't hurt me,' he cried, 'and I will give you gold.' At that moment a neighbour passed and called out: 'Where?' The man, hiding his face, pointed up to a box. The neighbour took the money, left. The man got up again."

WHEN HE ARRIVED, she lay upon the
bed. The washing of the body was finished. The room
was very dark. A ring of women circled her; Anna-Maria
sat. Two candles burned above the bed, above the place
of death; they would burn forty days. The doors and
shutters had been painted black.

"I used to tell you trouble, trouble, and you gave comfort."

He put his hand upon his mouth and breathed air from
his hand. He tried to smell his hand. A near woman hic-
cupped. He breathed air out again.

"Black are the clothes I wear, black is my heart also.
A fire in my breast is black smoke, blackened pain."

Orsetta was laid out in a shroud of grey and yellow-
white. No scissor and no needle had been used; the holes
for head and arms were burned. Her face was wetted once
with cotton wool and wine; her face was very white. A

waxen cross was placed inside her mouth, an ikon in her hand.

"May you not suffer another misfortune," people said to him. "May you never be left alone again."

"This, and no more," he said. "This, and no more."

"I thought to see you here for feasting, and it is a fast."

The women fingered beads, and bowed, and placed their wet hands on his face; the women all wore black. Alexis Panayotis stood within the door. Sotiris saw the table, and the ground beneath. He walked across the room.

"May you not suffer another misfortune; may your cares be mine," he said to Anna-Maria. "May you never once be left alone again."

She twisted a white kerchief in her hands and sucked at a brown bag suspended from her neck. She spoke to him, and as she spoke, the bag dropped free and banged against her breast. The bag was very wet. It held two coins, grains of salt, and charcoal, kept Signor Smith and all other spirits away; she always carried it.

"Orsetta died last night," Anna-Maria said. "Today is her birthday."

She sucked on the brown bag as if it were a pipe.

"Yayá," Sotiris said, "she died two nights ago."

Anna-Maria twisted her kerchief. She wiped herself with the brown lucky bag.

"Today Orsetta should have lived," she said. "Today is her birthday. I had a present for her, such a pretty shawl."

The women crowded to him, welcoming, beating their hands on thighs. They said it was an omen he had come, a happy death for her.

He stepped toward the bed. Orsetta's hair was badly matted, badly combed. Her face was very small, her neck a chicken's neck.

"I will become sweet air to enter in the tomb, to see if your white face is growing gray."

Her arms were sheathed; her feet he could not see. She lay a little crooked on the bed; he looked at the pillow. He wondered when the coffin would arrive.

"She could not die until you chose to come," the women said. "You made her dying sweet."

"This, and no more," they said.

The coffin had arrived. He heard some men outside, then bright light cut across the room, the door was opened suddenly, and Panayotis whispered in his ear:

"It is waiting outside."

"All right," Sotiris said. "Bring Ioannidis and one other man. We have to place her in."

The singsong quieted. Anna-Maria said: "You should have lived today. I broke a water jug."

"I used to tell you trouble, trouble, and you gave comfort. Please, close the room with bolts of silver that she may remain."

Then Panayotis left. He heard the noise outside. The women sang, and fingered beads; Anna-Maria sucked. Her stockings had blue flowers, and an ornamental vase. He breathed into his hand, looked round the single room at bayonet and photograph, the candlelit ikon.

"Close the room with bolts of silver, that she may remain."

Ioannidis, Panayotis, and a man he did not know carried

the coffin in. Moving with great care, they placed it by the bed. Ioannidis took off the lid and placed it by the wall; a woman closed the door, began to chant again:

"She suffered as the low stone of a mill."

Anna-Maria put her hand upon the coffin, felt the cloth, and started tearing it. She used both of her hands and fell; a woman raised her up.

"My door is dark as a black hen. No friends will come to visit now, only this sorrow."

Sotiris took a corner of the bed sheet; the three other men did the same. They lifted her from the bed; she slumped inward, askew.

Mistaken, still naming this her sister's festival day, Anna-Maria fell. A woman raised her up.

They laid Orsetta in the coffin, lowering the sheet. Because they did not touch her once, she settled crookedly.

"I shall take no more bread. I shall take your name only as my bread."

Sotiris knew that he would have to straighten her, and did. To move her arms and legs was difficult inside the shroud; he tried not to feel flesh.

"It is my grandmother," he thought. "Orsetta, yáya, you."

They folded the bed sheet across and covered her completely, placed the lid on top.

"Not a bad fit," Ioannidis decided, "not so bad at all." He imagined a sister inside. "Comfort yourselves," he said, "she has a smiling face."

"She died a smiling death."

Anna-Maria stroked her lucky bag. "Do you think so?"

she asked. "Her eyes were opened all last night; she must
have looked at me."

"She died two nights ago," Sotiris said again.

"I heard a hooting owl."

"I heard a wild dog cry."

Anna-Maria fell, and sat upon the floor. A woman tried
to help her, but she would not rise.

Sotiris tried to smell his hand, then took his hand away.
The room was very full, and hot. He saw the table, and
the black shell phonograph beneath. He saw the marble
Pan.

"In forty days I shall come to your grave, to see if your
high eyebrow has fallen. I will become sweet air to enter
in the tomb, to see if your white face is growing grey."

They bore the coffin out, balancing carefully, each man
holding a handle, Sotiris in front. The silver buckles of
the coffin glinted in the sun; he breathed fully again. Outside, a small crowd stood. Ioannidis took brass nails from
his pocket, and a large hammer. He placed them, one by
one, and Sotiris hammered, just lightly, just to hold the
top in place. A woman brought a wreath of flowers, white
and yellow, red. She placed it on the lid. She touched the
flowers and then turned away.

"I shall take no more bread. I shall take your name only
as my bread. Death is hard, the earth is heavy, and your
leaving is the heaviest of all."

Anna-Maria came to the black door. She held a glass
container in her hand, and with it sprinkled water and
rose water on the ground. The four men bore the coffin,
Sotiris in front, the length of the village. The women fol-

lowed, bent, beating their hands. And, as a prayer, no longer in song, they called out: "God forgive."

Sotiris watched the sea, the sand and truck. He felt the wooden walk but hardly felt the casket; it was very light. As the procession passed, water was sprinkled from each house, and from each house a woman called: "Forgive."

Anna-Maria came to them and touched the flower wreath. She kissed the coffin's side.

"How shall I say good-bye, how shall I take my leave, how say good-bye to you in the churchyard?"

The woman raised her up; they walked on to the truck. Ioannidis climbed in; Anna-Maria was handed up beside him; they would drive to the church. Everyone wanted to go with the truck, nobody wanted to walk. Sotiris asked the time.

"This, and no more," somebody said. "This, and no more."

"Past one o'clock," he heard. "We must go to the church."

"All right," Sotiris said. "Let us go, then."

They lifted up the coffin to the truck; it settled easily. Sotiris climbed up after it and said:

"I shall ride here alone." He pounded on the cabin window, called that they could go.

Ioannidis drove off. The other men started to run, or walk up to the church; some went back to their homes. The men all wore white shirts, black-banded, with no tie.

Sotiris hammered in the nails, hard, fully, all of them, so that the top was firm. Eleven nails he counted, in the sun. He hit the silver handles twice, making the handles ring. The truck moved heavily.

Stroking her lucky bag, Anna-Maria said:

"Women, can you tell me where your neighbour is? If she is in front, I shall wait there for her; if she is behind, I shall wait there also; if she be in the earth, I can no longer care."

Uncreased, his short legs lay before him, light blue, of a light weave, and the brown buckle shoes beneath a dark blue sock beat time to his mind's tune. He tried his lighter twice. "September twenty-third," he said, and wondered, was he right? He lit a cigarette; white clouds billowed below. He still could taste his egg.

Triphon turned to the window and half saw the sun on the wing; distorted, he stared back, flat in the window frame. "I am a traveller," he sang, "and you a railroad track." Strong-centered, silver-bright, the glistening of sun electrified the plane and needled light in lines. White clouds seemed cotton-soft. He rested his blue elbow on the pillow by his side and looked at the next seat. A pouch of postcards, information ("Flight and fright," his lawyer had said), and the bent disposal bag sagged underneath his book; he hooked a finger in the lining, yawned. Bought at the airport, with Bettina gone, after his second scotch, and when nobody looked, it had remained unread. He had fallen asleep. "Circus of Sin," the yellow letters said. A dwarf sat on a fat woman's shoulders, feet touching her one breast. A trapeze girl pranced past. Triphon revolved the book so that it faced the inside of the pouch; he tapped his cigarette. Red ash flaked to the floor.

Undone, his tie's two ends sighed touching as he turned. His lawyer sat beside, bifocal glasses low. Breakfast had been at eight. The plane dipped suddenly; his stomach rose and fell. "Are you asleep?" he asked, knowing his lawyer slept. Answered with only breath, he turned to the window again, and to his flattened face. A bit of bacon rind fell down across his suit. "Two hours still to go"— his hand fingered his chin—"and then from Athens to Rhodes." The trapeze girl, in black and white, reduced now, left alone, lifted her naked leg across the rear cover; he uncovered her ankle and her stationary foot. He rubbed his stomach roll. The stewardess walked past; he smoked and turned away.

"You have the legal right," his lawyer had proclaimed, black briefcase by his lap, "to order the house closed. Without a will, until such time as settlement is made, or until will be found ("No chance of that," Triphon had said, and asked him for the salt), you are an equal beneficiary with each and both of your brothers—the key is one-third yours."

His left leg was asleep; he stamped it into pain. His lawyer's lips hung slack. He wondered, should he shave? At home, his wife would also be asleep. And, hair in curlers, thin, his sister-in-law slept; the two women, together, in one room. "The milkman, now," he thought, "can take his little rest. And welcome, too," he thought, "to every egg you find." His sister-in-law had moved in to stay; they had a twelve-room house.

Triphon was fifty-nine. He owned a factory for making paper plates. He ate off paper plates for lunch and drank from paper cups. He had blue-purple eyes and watched them in his knife. His secretary, Bettina, ate every lunch with him.

"Think of the carob tree," he thought, "and my last trip to Rhodes. Four years ago, merely."

He wondered, was this land? He ringed with smoke the button blowing air, and he decided, no.

The white church of Malona, with one dome and one surmounting cross, sat up above the little square, on a high piling of stone. It shadowed a stopped fountain and long empty gutters, a broken walk of stone. Jolting on cobbles, the truck came to a stop. Sotiris helped Anna-Maria into the center of the church, holding her round the waist. Apelis and Andreas had arrived; formally, they greeted him, and greeted Anna-Maria. Sotiris returned to the door.

Men like migrant birds came quickly to the square, coming from alleyways and gathering beneath. Sotiris helped them bring the coffin in; they bore it slowly up the steps and placed it on a table, in the center of the church, before the ikonostási and the Holy Door. The church was but one room. They placed four candles round the coffin as a cross, each villager lighting his own small candle from the flame. Men and women mingled, because the church was small, arching out around the table, waiting for the priests. Children, wearing white, stared at the small black box. Wide-eyed, one girl sat down, in a wooden seat by the wall.

"You cannot sit," her mother said. "You must stand up, or kneel."

"This, and no more," the people said, holding their candles out. And then the priests arrived.

The elder priest had grey hair, and the younger, black. Their beards were very long, the grey one and the black; their hair, beneath the caps, piled high. The younger, second priest went to the table of oblation, took the censer up, blessed the coffin and the mourners, initiated song.

The church was almost cold. High windows filtered in the light, but, even so, the chandeliers were lit, two high glass chandeliers, ornate, covered in plastic for cleanliness' sake and to preserve the glass. When, twice a year, the plastic bubble was removed, by workmen, for high services, the workmen came down coated with white dust. A lamp of olive oil was lit; the bell had ceased to toll.

Sotiris held his candle in both hands, and held it forward, out; he was surrounded by the villagers, and the curious of Malona, whom he did not know. Anna-Maria stood across the coffin lid; Stavros, in the dark background, stood apart.

The Bible and the sponge, the seven-branched candelabra, caught reflected light. Sotiris rubbed his left pant leg with his right instep.

"O Holy God, Holy Mighty, Holy Immortal One, have mercy upon us."

"Upon us each and all," Sotiris was forced to repeat, and all the children of the classroom laughed. He stood straining after words, the vowel after vowel, ferocious, eight years old, and wished completely, white-faced, for release. Upon us each and all, he said, six times toward the class.

"With the souls of the righteous dead, give rest, O Saviour," sang the priests, "to the soul of Thy servant, Orsetta Procopirios." Anna-Maria, too, intoned; she knew the service all by heart. "Preserving her unto the life of blessedness which is with Thee, O Thou who lovest mankind."

A small boy to Sotiris' right was told to swing the censer; he swung it in rhythm, tapping to keep time.

"Into the place of Thy rest, O Lord, where all Thy Saints repose, give rest also to the soul of Thy servant, Orsetta Procopirios, for Thou alone lovest mankind."

He swung it happily, the thick smoke coming fast. "Unburdened as I am, repeat and follow me." "Unburdened as I am," Sotiris told his teacher, and the laughing class.

The white floor of the church was cold; the mourners shuffled feet. Sotiris, looking down, saw a thin edge of sheet snaked out beneath the coffin top, and realized he must have wedged it in while hammering. White lip in a black mouth, he wanted it to speak.

"More honourable than the Cherubim, and beyond compare more glorious than the Seraphim, Thou who without defilement barest God, the Word, true Birth Giver of God, we magnify Thee, Lord, have mercy, Lord."

"Fidelity," Sotiris said three hundred times to earth and fingered a tin can. His father's cave was dark.

Hot wax dripped to his hand; he looked around again. Near him, and to the left, a woman mourner stood; she had one eye of glass. Her good eye was in water from the smoke, her glass eye glinted in the light. The smell was very strong; he looked at the white edge of sheet, a rivulet in black. Apelis smiled at him; Andreas did the same. "Fidelity," he thought, and, silent, said the word.

"Blessed are those that are undefiled in the way and walk in the law of the Lord. Allelujah. Blessed are they that keep His testimonies, and seek Him with their whole heart, for they who do no wickedness, walk in His ways."

He wondered which of the two priests was in league with Triphon, and which with his father.

Manos stood very near. His tight black coat was wet. Sotiris moved his hands. Bereft, good, garrulous, Manos began to cry.

> *A boat from Crete*
> *not big, not small*
> *but fifty cubits long*
> *casts anchor*
> *here at Rhodes.*

"Give rest also to the soul of Thy servant, both now and ever."

The metal of the censer jarred and scraped; the boy swung it too high, too freely. The black-haired priest stepped forward, not interrupting his chant, catching the boy's arm.

"I hope," Sotiris thought, "it is the grey-haired one we've bribed."

The boy jangled less loudly; Stavros, behind, held out his shepherd's crook. His face was shadowed, high, held above the light.

"Establish her into Thy courts, as it is written, regarding not, in that Thou art good, her sins, whether voluntary or involuntary, and all things committed, either with knowledge or in ignorance, O Thou who lovest mankind."

Anna-Maria, he could see, was crying without noise and plucking at the lucky bag held underneath her chin. Tears travelled the crisscrossing of her skin, the labyrinth of her face, spongelike and glistening, near-blind. He wanted to reach out, and, moving, almost shook his candle dead. He thought about Dania.

Apelis, in black suit, with bowed head lit by the flame that he held, old-seeming, leonine, stood very straight; Sotiris straightened too.

"Give rest to the soul of Thy departed servant, Orsetta Procopirios, in a place of brightness, a place of verdure, a place of repose, whence all sickness, sorrow, and sighing have fled away."

On mountains the thistle grows,
your words were honey.

"How much more time," Sotiris thought, and listened to the priest, "till all of this is done?"

Anna-Maria started to collapse. A woman held her up;

the priest retired through the Holy Door. The boy did not stop with his incense, and the priest returned. Behind Sotiris, to the left, the one door of the church stood open, and there strong sunlight entered, dust dancing in the beams.

"Pardon every transgression, which she hath committed, whether by word, or deed, or thought. For Thou art a good God and lovest mankind; because there is no man who liveth and sinneth not; for Thou only art without sin, and Thy righteousness is to all eternity, and Thy word is true."

The two priests sang in unison; the woman mourner by his side stuffed garlic in her nose. Her good eye was in water from the incense, her glass eye staring at the sun.

"My father's one mother," Sotiris told himself and touched the coffin gently with his knee.

"For she hath vanished from among her kind, and presseth onward to the grave, and vexeth herself no longer concerning vanities, and concerning the flesh, which suffereth sore distress. Where are now her kinsfolk and her friends? Lo, we are parted, let us beseech the Lord that He will give her rest."

Sotiris saw the children stamping feet: Anna-Maria fell.

"We pardon thee, O spiritual Child, all thy deeds done amiss in this life, both voluntary and involuntary, now and ever, and unto ages of ages. Amen."

The priests retired, and the singing stopped. All deeds, he told himself, she did amiss were pardoned, and her

legacy was love. Still holding his candle, he crossed to
Anna-Maria, stooped to help her rise. Crumpled, holding
her black soiled dress and stomach, blowing through her
nose, she blew at the candle he held, a yellow stain spreading beneath her on the floor.

Upon the market paving, a basket full of fish stood open
to the air, and someone dropped a slice of melon in. The
owner laughed and laughed. Dania held tightly to her
shopping bag and moved along the stalls, in the open
market, buying food. She bought bananas, meat and
grapes, bread loaves and barboúnia; Mehmet deserved a
treat. She did not bargain long; she did it only as a gesture,
knowing she overpaid. Once someone had asked a hundred
drachmas for a ceramic jug, and she had said, no, I'll give
you forty drachmas, and he had answered, yes, and, surprised, she had paid, and taken it, and it was broken,
cracked. "But Sotiris might come," she thought, and,
therefore, bought new wine.

"He's changed," she told herself, and disregarded pears.
"He is always with me," she thought. "He was lost, and is
found."

Standing beside the truck, in sun, Sotiris watched the
procession begin to file toward the graveyard, black and
brightly lit, the women following. His father and his
brother walked ahead; he bent to take his coat; a lizard
sunned itself on the warm fountain wall. He looked at the
emerald lizard, the dry fountain, the stones, the dust upon
his feet. He started to follow the coffin and the mourning

group; Triphon would soon arrive, would purchase, bring a spade. A bird spiralled through sky.

Stand anywhere within the streets of Rhodes. Beneath there sounds the sea. Above, if it is nighttime, not a festive day, the mountain shelters homeless Signor Smith. Out of diamonds he would make coal.